COFFEE KILLED MY MOTHER

Coffee Killed My Mother

A novel

by

DONNA STRAMELLA

Adelaide Books
New York/Lisbon
2020

COFFEE KILLED MY MOTHER
A novel
By Donna Stramella

Copyright © by Donna Stramella
Cover design © 2020 Adelaide Books

Published by Adelaide Books, New York / Lisbon
adelaidebooks.org
Editor-in-Chief
Stevan V. Nikolic

For any information, please address Adelaide Books
at info@adelaidebooks.org
or write to:
Adelaide Books
244 Fifth Ave. Suite D27
New York, NY, 10001

ISBN-10: 1-951896-38-6
ISBN-13: 978-1-951896-38-6

Printed in the United States of America

To Tony with love

Contents

Prologue

The worst part was my feet got cut, or maybe it was getting lost in my own neighborhood, or not helping my mother? Probably the worst–I was going to die.

Before my feet got cut, I was lost, couldn't help my mother, and was ready to die, I heard a loud crash. It reminded me of the year before, when I tried to pull the yellow rose (the rest were all gold) from the vase on the table, and crash—it all fell on the kitchen floor. My mother was mad at first, but when I started to cry she pulled out the broom and said, "The floor needs a good sweep anyway," and then she started to sing about red roses and a blue lady even though the roses were yellow and gold.

This new crash was so loud it woke me. Barefoot on the wood floor, there was a crack of light from the broken window shade to show me that one piece of rough wood. That piece once left a splinter in my leg while I read a book on the floor. I also saw a lump resting against my dresser that I knew was my kindergarten backpack. My mother let me pick it out from It Bears Repeating, the store with the giant teddy bear. When my new friend Sadie said she liked the backpack, I could feel my smile stretch. When I told her where I got it, Sadie scrunched up her face and said, "That's other peoples' stuff," and walked away. I watched her long blonde curls go up and down until she turned into our classroom.

That happened just the week before, a new memory. When I die, I won't have any new memories.

The light in the living room was a little brighter. My mother slept on the couch, face to the wall, arm pointing down and I followed it to the floor and saw the glass.

I shook her shoulder, then rubbed her back. "Mom, Mom? Wake up. Can you wake up?" Next to the tall bottle on the coffee table, I saw her phone. I pressed the start button. Dead battery. Again.

There was the sound of leaves rustling and I felt cool air. The front door was open. Maybe my mother couldn't call 911 because of the dead battery. Maybe she was going to get help but felt weak and had to lie down. That happened sometimes. My mother never wanted me to get help. Except this time she wouldn't wake up to tell me.

I stepped over two big pieces of glass. As I put my foot down I felt little stabs at the bottom and top of my foot, like shots from the doctor that made me cry. I wanted to cry even as I kept walking and felt tiny pinches each time a foot touched the floor. Outside the air felt colder than it did earlier when my mother walked me home from school. It looked different too. I didn't remember where the friendly people lived. The lady who let me pet her dog Ollie. The man who sat on his step with the newspaper and said, "Good day ladies" when he saw us. I couldn't see the color of the houses in the dark.

On our cement porch, my feet started to hurt more. I didn't want to think about my feet anymore so I kept walking and started counting houses. I was up to 12 and not a single house looked friendly. I started shaking. I needed a friendly house so I could knock on the door and ask a friendly person to help my mother.

The shadow on house 13 looked like a dragon. On house 18, a bird with a single giant wing. I turned and turned again. House 25 had no shadow but I could hear a dog barking—not Ollie. At house 28, I knew I was lost. At house 29 I knew I was going to die. If I didn't find help before I died no one would wake my mother.

The shadows were speaking, telling me this place was safe in the light, but not in the dark. In the light I held my mother's hand when we walked to kindergarten on the days when she got up on time. In the light we went trick or treating on Halloween, then my mother picked through my candy for her favorites. In the light I watched other children play outside while my mother napped in her room.

Not a single friendly house but I found a friendly tree with low branches to hide me as I died. And even though my feet still hurt, I could feel my body rest.

I don't remember dreaming that night, but I do remember the morning light that told me I didn't die. The leaves above me were all green, but many different greens. I wanted to stay and count how many greens until I thought about my mother.

The light led me in the right direction as I counted each house. I wasn't sure at first, but when I saw the house with the dragon shadow—now gone–I knew I was on my way home.

When I left, I closed the door without locking. If the door was locked that meant my mother woke up and pushed in the button. I took a deep breath, my hand on the handle. *Please be locked*. But it turned and I slowly pushed the door open. The glass was still on the floor but the couch was empty. The water was running in the bathroom and my mother hummed a song. She didn't hear me. Didn't know I almost died.

After I'm in bed, I wondered if I dreamt it all. Maybe my mother wasn't sick. Maybe I didn't get lost and almost die. Then I felt my hurt feet.

Chapter 1

My mother has no sense of direction.

I arrived at birthday parties, the shiny paper and bows in a tussle on the floor while kids with icing-frosted lips played with the red firetrucks or Barbie dolls. I never sang the Happy Birthday song or watched my friends blow out the candles.

For a full month, I imagined riding a pony at my friend, Cindy's party. Her grandmother who was flying in from Dallas promised to rent a pony for her granddaughter's 8th birthday. When we arrived, I saw the long tail hanging over the half-door of the trailer, just as it pulled out of the driveway. Cindy's cowgirl hat was tilted to one side as she waved goodbye to the worn-out pony.

I was always the last player at field hockey practices and games, taking extra laps in the afternoon heat and humidity to compensate for tardiness, the rest of the team sitting beneath a shade tree in the cool grass, eating juicy, ice-cold orange slices.

Once, we were even later than our usual half-hour to 45-minutes "make an entrance time" my mother mentioned whenever I complained. This time it was the funeral of Mr. McGregor, my white-haired American History teacher who died of a heart attack at school, right in the middle of our studies on the Great Depression. He had just introduced Roosevelt's

New Deal when he stopped talking, stared straight ahead and opened his eyes wide. One hand rested on his chest, the other on the edge of his desk when he fell to the dirty gray tile floor.

My mother insisted no one arrived at funerals on time, but as we parked and raced toward the tented area at the gravesite, the punctual mourners were already returning to their cars. The prayers had been recited, veteran's flag presented, flowers tossed on the coffin, and tears shed. This time, I didn't mind being late. Funerals were my least favorite obligation.

Today, my mother's shortcoming puts us 60 miles from our target destination. That's what I get for falling asleep. I scroll through Google images on my phone, looking at pictures of Hanover, Pennsylvania—this is not the view outside my car window. No fields of bright yellow and cornflower blue wildflowers. No Amish farmers in horse-drawn buggies. No black and white cows grazing near red barns. No historic buildings. No Utz Factory Tour.

The only thing that helped me get out of bed this morning, to start our drive from Northern Beach, New Jersey was the promise of Utz potato chips. Even now, I imagine the sweet smell just inside the factory, the lightly oiled, salty coating playing on my tongue. Even in the wrong Hanover, I can almost taste the delicate curled snack when I lick my lips.

We exit slowly off the highway, the ramp tight with cars. Immediately, we are crushed by buildings—not quaint historic row houses or wooden barns–but restaurants, stores, an outlet mall, and even a casino. A giant screen on the side of the casino flashes advertisements: $100,000 pay off! Win a Lexus!! Sunday—Ravens Football on the big screen!!!

We're now in Hanover, Maryland, an unexpected first stop on what my mother calls our "Coffee by Car" trip to visit as many coffee shops as possible. I'm 17, and instead of working at the sandwich shop near my house, grilling porta-bellas and chopping onions and zucchinis while I think about where I'll eventually enroll in college, this is my life—at least for the next several months. In texts with friends, I call the journey "Coffee with Crazy."

The trip had been sparked by a comment in a blog my mother followed. A blog about coffee and people who loved coffee. A blog about people like my mother. The writer described Fairyland Coffee in Hanover, Pennsylvania as *impossibly tiny on the outside and stocked with five times the goodness inside. A fairy tale cottage with a bottomless carafe of coffee.*

Fairy Tale. Bottomless. My mother was going to get there. Only, she wasn't—at least not now.

My 61-year-old mother has always been a bit eccentric. A white woman who wears her shoulder-length blonde hair in cornrows, her pale skin looks sallow with her bright red lipstick. She has loved red for as long as I can remember. Her bedroom has a red accent wall and our flower garden has at least five varieties of red rose bushes. With her slim figure, she could wear fitted dresses. Instead, her messy closet holds flowing clothes in large, bright floral-prints in every shade of red and pink.

She shops at two second-hand stores in our town, and her visits are so frequent that the owners hold clothes behind the counter that fit her preferred profile. The merchandise is already cheap, but my mother gets a frequent shopper discount at both places, and she's sure to thank the owners with occasional cups of their favorite coffees. For Marlissa, the chatty red-headed owner of It Bears Repeating: a double espresso mocha. For Isabella, the owner of Second Skin who intersperses Spanish expressions in her conversation: a vanilla latte with skim. My mother determined that Second Skin merchandise was the less expensive of the two based solely on a single fact. During the same week, she saw identical red Chico's skirts—one in each shop. The price was fifty-cents more at It Bears Repeating.

I was born to a 44-year-old single mother.

"I'd flat out given up," she'd tell me every year on my birthday. "I desperately wanted a child but was never blessed that way. Imagine my joy! And having a girl was the icing on the cake!"

A short, round brunette, I look like my father, which means I am the exact opposite of my tall, slender blonde mother—with one exception.

"Anna Lee," she'd say. "Do you know how blessed you are that God gave you my blue eyes? And with your brown hair and long eyelashes people notice them even more."

It's true, her eyes are lovely. Sometimes, I look up at her and see a soft blue reflection. Other times, I see an approaching storm, the blue waves churning and heading in my direction. Today, I see clouds. Clouds of confusion.

"This doesn't look historic," she says, the clouds forming in her eyes. "It doesn't look rural either."

My eyes roll back.

"Could you check the map on your phone?" she asks. "Maybe I took the wrong exit."

My eyes roll back further.

"Or maybe I just need to drive to the other side of that mall."

Now my eyes are rolling around inside my head. In protest, I hadn't said a word since we left the driveway, but I can't hold back any longer.

"You're in the wrong state," I say, the corners of my mouth curling up in angry amusement.

She looks straight ahead, her red lips pursed.

"Humor isn't helpful," she says and keeps driving.

"I'm not being humorous. But you're being wrong. Again."

Like always, I want to say more. Instead I start counting the places lined up on the boulevard. There are four salons—three for nails and one for hair; a total of seven restaurants serving seafood and steak, burritos and burgers, pizza and pasta; six stores selling beds, cards, candles, cell phones, groceries.

I hear the evenly spaced click, click, click of the blinker as we turn off the main road. In the distance, there are two hotels, surrounded by young trees on the brink of new colors. The sun is setting on a deep blue early autumn sky and Hanover reveals some natural beauty for the first time since we took the exit. The pure white clouds from a minute ago are now rimmed in pink.

We pass a simple, white clapboard church, large pots of yellow mums on both sides of the entrance. Above the shiny black door, the steeple rises, the bell reflecting the pink and blue above.

Our aging Jeep Wrangler—red paint peeling over dents that were never fixed and with the odometer hovering not far from 200,000—turns into the first hotel parking lot.

"Can't you just smell the coffee in the air?" she smiles. "I have a good feeling about Hanover."

We are traveling light, one large roller bag each. My mother is certain most hotels will have a washer and dryer.

"Just like we're backpacking across Europe," she told me as we packed.

But without backpacks. And without Europe.

A few brown leaves crunch beneath my flip flops—autumn's early notice. If my mother keeps driving south, we'll miss it.

As the automatic hotel doors open, I smell the roasted beans I know so well. Not because I drink the stuff, but because my mother consumes up to 10 cups a day. At home, the smell is everywhere—in the kitchen of course—but also in the bedroom where she sits in bed to drink her first cup of the day, her office where she taps out stories for the local newspaper, the foyer where she continually sloshes the overfilled contents on the carpet when she answers the door, and even my room where she invites herself in to sit on the edge of my bed and ask about my day.

At the hotel courtesy counter with two big aluminum containers, she is already turning the lever, a steaming brown river of life flowing into her cardboard cup. She takes a sip, tilting her head back slightly and closing her eyes.

I straddle my bag, rolling it back and forth with my feet as my mother heads to the check-in desk.

The older man behind the counter asks, "How may I help you?"

"My daughter and I would like a room for the night."

"Do you have a reservation?" he asks, playing with the end of his thick gray mustache.

I get off my luggage and make a slow circle around the lobby, passing the cramped business center with a single computer and printer, the steamy window with a view of the indoor pool that has fake palm trees in each far corner, and a tiny gift shop that is unmanned at the moment.

At the end of the circle, my mother's standing by our luggage.

"Here's one for you" she says, handing me a key card. "Guess what? We ARE in the wrong state!"

I shake my head, wondering if this first miscalculation is an omen for the rest of our trip. A trip that I tried unsuccessfully to avoid, even suggesting I stay with my father. It was torture to stay with him for a weekend. Yet I was willing to spend months mostly alone in his sprawling rancher while he worked 12-hour days. Definitely a more tolerable option than sharing hotel rooms and long drives with my mother.

Last night in my own bed for what I knew would be some time, I could feel myself drifting off immediately, dreaming I was sitting comfortably in the Adirondack chair behind my father's waterfront house, the lake perfectly still, reflecting red and yellow maples and tall long-needled pine trees on the banks. The sun shone directly above, a whisper of a breeze on my face to balance the Indian summer temperatures. The air was scented with a familiar sweet smell—honeysuckle or maybe lilac. In the stillness I heard a soft buzz, the sound growing louder and louder until it filled my ears. I swatted at the insect but the noise continued.

"Anna Lee! Anna Lee," it buzzed. "ANNA LEE! ANNA LEE!"

I opened my eyes. Those garish yellow braids were just inches from my face.

"It's time to start our adventure!"

Chapter 2

She slips the key card into the door and it blinks red. Undeterred, she taps it back with her "candy red" index fingernail, then tries a third time.

I don't want to make life easier for her, but I don't want to wait in the narrow hall, further crowded with housekeeping carts and piles of dirty linens.

"Let me try," I say, pulling my key card out of my pocket.

The light blinks green, and I turn the handle to enter.

"Yes, it's that easy," I say with an exaggerated sigh.

There's the instant smell of freshness—a mixture of pine and floral bar soap with bits of lemon.

She opens the shades to a darkening sky to see the view, or the lack of one. There is no lake reflecting the moon. No view of a back lit Utz sign. The only lights are from the retail, restaurants and casino of the wrong Hanover.

"Let's freshen up and get something to eat," she says.

I pick up the remote on the table and leave my neon green flip flops on the floor, sitting back on one of the two Queen beds and adjusting three pillows behind me, which feels like a luxury. At home I have one hopelessly flat pillow. I aimlessly scroll through the selections on the flat screen—even more of a luxury compared to the clunky, castoff TV from our neighbor—so heavy it took three people to move it into our living room.

My mother leaves her empty coffee cup with the red lipstick print next to the screen, opens her suitcase, pulls out her makeup bag, and starts to sing. The only words I can make out are *sunshine* and *coffee*. Probably one of the many impromptu songs she composes for even the most obscure situations. Her voice rises louder each time she hits the word *coffee*. It's a prominent word in the song.

If a genie appeared from a bottle at that moment and granted me one wish, I'd ask him to cut out her vocal cords—swiftly and completely. In truth, her voice was fine. The problem was the frequency. She sang when she put on her makeup, drove in the car, poured herself a cup of coffee, cleaned the house.

I turn up the volume on an episode of "The Big Bang Theory" that I'd already seen a few times. Penny and Sheldon pair up for a scavenger hunt and are putting a puzzle together for the first clue. Penny figures out the answer quickly, but her teammate insists on putting all the pieces together before they leave. They are the last to arrive at the Comic Book Store.

"I love this episode," she smiles, emerging from the bathroom. "Penny and Sheldon are on an adventure like us!"

She returns the rose-colored makeup bag edged with pink sparkles to her suitcase and calls the front desk.

"Is there a local coffee shop in the area? One that serves food?"

She picks up the hotel-provided pen and notepad from the desk and writes.

"Do you know what time they close?"

She finishes her call and turns in my direction.

"Good news—there's a place nearby where we can get coffee and a late dinner—wraps, salads, soups."

I stare at the screen.

"We'll need to get moving–they close in 45 minutes."

I try to imagine myself in the Adirondack chair. The lake illuminated by a full moon, the breeze soft on my skin. Crickets chirping in the distance. And then there's the buzz.

"Anna Lee, ANNA LEE."

I know the buzzing won't stop, so I toss the remote on the bed, open up my suitcase, and pull out my own makeup bag—no glitter. Inside the bathroom, I turn on the fan, close the toilet lid, sit down and begin scrolling through my phone. About 15 minutes pass before the buzzing starts again.

"Are you almost finished?" she shouts above the fan.

"Not yet," I shout back, continuing to watch a video on my phone that shows stupid people doing stupid things—a guy pulling another guy on a sled behind his truck, a woman trying to do a black flip into a pool that ends with her hitting the side, two kids colliding on a trampoline and falling off the edge. I'm pulling up more videos, and hoping unrealistically they'll somehow prevent her from knocking on the door. It's been a total of 25 minutes, so I'll just need to stall for another 10 or so. Another knock—this time much louder.

"Almost ready," I shout back, turning on the water in the sink, then text a couple of my friends. No response.

I check the time on my phone before I finally emerge from the bathroom. My mother is sitting on the other bed, putting on another layer of red lipstick, looking in a small hand mirror. She snaps it shut, closes the lipstick and looks up.

"The bad news is, we're too late for the coffee shop. But the good news is, we passed a Sunrise Sprinkles where we can grab a breakfast sandwich."

I consider reminding her that our trip is about independent coffee shops, not big franchises. I shake my head slowly.

"No Sunrise Sprinkles for me. I'm not feeling so well," I say, putting my hand on my stomach to really sell my excuse.

Back on the bed, I look for the remote before I see it in her hand. With an exaggerated gesture, she stands up, clicks the television off, then closes her eyes and tilts back her head before placing the remote on the nightstand. I know she can already smell the coffee, and she gives me a sideward glance as she leaves. Not even a goodbye, which is fine. Maybe if she gets annoyed with me she'll cut the trip short.

I turn the TV back on and pull out my new journal from the suitcase—a gift from my mother for the trip.

"To chronicle our journey," she told me.

"Why would anyone use a paper journal?" I argued. "Only old people use paper journals."

"You need to feel the pen in your hand. That's where creativity starts."

The journal's cover features a large, teal coffee mug. The brown contents form a swirl that rises above the mug and splits in two. At the top of the cover, the swirls reunite and form a heart.

I reach over to the nightstand and grab the hotel pen, sitting for a moment, waiting for inspiration. I'm ready. On the first page, in large, swirled handwriting inspired by the cover, I write: *100 Reasons Why My Mother is Crazy.*

Flipping the page, I continue: *#1 – She drove to the wrong state.*

I could easily fill up all 100 slots in a single night but decide to focus the journal on the trip, just as my mother suggested. Besides, coming up with 100 previous examples of her craziness would be too easy—like during my first year of middle school.

At Douglas Regional, there was a tradition of celebrating spirit week, encouraging students to break convention, but only in an approved, unified manner. I was already embarrassed each morning when my mother insisted on parking in the lot, then walking me to the door, while most other parents just waited in the car line and dropped their now independent middle schoolers in front of the building.

I should have realized that spirit week would be something my mother couldn't resist. Something so absurd that she couldn't possibly leave it for the middle schoolers.

"Oh, Anna Lee. I'm going to get onboard the spirit train!"

My pleas that school spirit week was reserved for people actually enrolled in the school were ignored. For a full two weeks prior, a feeling of dread started to build, like when we turned the calendar to a new month and I saw an upcoming dental appointment. I kept hoping my fears wouldn't be realized.

Monday was "Crazy Hair Day." Lucky for me, her long, tiny braids were crazy already, so she wore a short, blonde wig that almost made her look normal. She borrowed the wig from our neighbor Liz who was just finishing her chemo.

Tuesday was "Inside Out Day." Lucky again. The bright flowers on her flowing dresses were nicely muted when she turned her dress inside out.

My luck was over by Wednesday. "Pajama Day." She wore a long, red-checkered flannel nightgown that she bought at Second Skin for $3.50. As if the walk to the front of the school wasn't humiliating enough, the photographer from the local paper where she worked met us at the flagpole for a picture. My mother wrote a piece about Spirit Week and the Northern Beach Gazette ran the photo. I could see my fellow students laughing in the background.

On "Tacky Thursday" and "Crazy Sock Friday" I was sick. Too sick for school. I used the same hand-on-the-stomach technique to convince her, and she believed me. But by the time Spirit Week rolled around the next year, she knew the truth. I told her I'd be sick for the entire week if she insisted on dressing up. She'd already shown me her new plan for crazy hair, which included rainbow feathers and pink sparkle spray.

"You don't want me to have any fun," she pouted.

There were other school examples I could use for my journal as well. In second grade, she wrote an end-of-year rap song and convinced the principal to let her sing it over the morning announcements. Thankfully, my classmates were talking during the announcements, and our teacher didn't care—there were only a few hours standing in the way of her own summer break and by the time the new school year rolled around, my mother's rap was forgotten.

For our fourth-grade class trip to the zoo, my mother dressed up like a lion, and only removed the headpiece after the faux fur around her face started sticking to her skin in the late spring heat.

More recently, she saw me at the beach one day after school. My friends, two girls, two guys, were sitting around a picnic table on the grassy section that fronted our community beach. Everyone was talking about their upcoming moves into their dorms, or in my case, which college I might eventually attend. One that was far, far away from New Jersey. And then I saw her walking straight toward us, her braids swaying, her multicolored floral cover up flowing in the slight breeze.

"How many of you are sexually active?" she asked, immediately followed by, "Are you using protection?"

Everyone just stared in silence until she finally walked away without a response. Unless you count my silent "Really?" directed with the most lethal stare I could manage under the circumstances. If my friends were pressed to answer the second question, they'd all nod their heads, but based on what I'd heard over the last couple of years, they'd probably be lying. The first question was easier to answer. It was a yes, for everyone but me.

It was an overcast day, but the heat on my face was never more intense. Thinking back, it was twofold—a combination of embarrassment and anger. It didn't help that later, my friends told other people who weren't even there. I kept hoping one of their mothers would do something even more embarrassing so everyone would move on to a new story. Except my friends' mothers actually thought about their kids' feelings.

And, if my journal wasn't specific to the trip, I would add the craziest thing my mother ever did. In retrospect, it bordered on psychotic. It was the time she tried to destroy my father's wedding.

Chapter 3

My mother never married—not before I was born, not after. My father was married just once—to my mother's best friend.

I was 4-years-old. The wedding was my earliest memory, one that was unfortunately seared into my mind. When I think of that day, my skin starts to itch. I wore a stiff white dress with a wide bright pink silk ribbon around my waist and carried a little white basket filled with pink rose petals.

I looked down at my shiny white shoes, glitter accents on the straps, as I carefully placed one foot in front of the other, just like I practiced. I remember the pink rose pedals felt like velvet as I dropped them one by one on the white carpet strip that ran down the aisle. I stood beside my father at the front of the altar and turned as the organist played "Here Comes the Bride."

In her lacy white gown, Miss June walked down the aisle slowly. A few feet behind her, a woman followed in a long black dress, her face covered by a thin black veil. Unaware of the shadow behind her, Miss June looked glamorous, her usually straight red hair fashioned in loose curls. She turned from side-to-side, smiling at the wedding guests. About midway up the aisle the veiled woman seated herself at the end of an empty row.

Miss June was at the front standing next to my father, whose face was scrunched with worry. He pulled the handkerchief, just made for show, out of his front pocket and blotted his face. As the minister began to speak, I heard a woman crying—quietly at first, then breaking into loud sobs. The woman pulled the veil back from her face—it was my mother.

There was a slight gasp from Miss June, and I looked up at my father. He nodded at two men seated near the front, and I watched them as they moved toward my mother. My heart started beating fast, my palms sweaty—feelings that I've come to know well over the years. My mother walked out with the men and I heard her sobs until they shut the double doors at the entrance. The men stood guard there for the rest of the short ceremony. I can't remember if I cried. I do remember I wanted to run outside with my mother. Instead, I stared my shiny white shoes, pressed close together.

I close my eyes and think about that day and remember my time with Miss June. She was always kind to me when I stayed at my father's house. She did not wear her hair in long braids. She did not wear dresses that were two sizes too large. She did not embarrass me.

Miss June and my father were married five years. After the divorce, she moved to Arizona to live near her family, and I never saw her again.

Chapter 4

All those memories must have lulled me to sleep. I'm still holding the pen when I'm startled awake by a whirling noise. My phone shows I've been sleeping for nearly three hours, and my mother has not returned. The noise is outside, and I look out in time to see a helicopter flying toward the mall.

I can see the hotel parking lot from the room, and the space where we parked is empty. I'm determined not to call her.

The TV is still on, and the 11:00 news is starting. The lead story is a fatal stabbing, and I realize the helicopter that just flew over the hotel is hovering above a shopping center now, the cameraman focusing on one of the buildings below. And then I see it—Sunrise Sprinkles. I hear a woman talking, and they've cut to a shot of the reporter at ground level, with the building some distance behind her.

"We have few details to report, but here's what we know," she says speaking quickly, looking down at her notepad. "A customer entered the store and found a woman on the floor who had been stabbed multiple times. The victim has not been identified, but she was pronounced dead on the scene. The police will provide her name once the next of kin has been identified."

In the background, I see our red Jeep in the parking lot.

Immediately, I call my mother. The phone goes directly to voice mail—typical, since she rarely turns on her cell. I send her a text: CALL ME.

My heart is beating fast, my mouth so dry it's hard to swallow. I force myself to drink some water as I watch the rest of the news, hoping for an update, but the anchors are talking about zoning enforcement in Annapolis, two daytime shootings in Baltimore, the unseasonably warm weather, the final series for Orioles baseball, and predictions for Sunday's Ravens game.

I look out the window again. In the distance, I still see the helicopter. There are deep shadows across the roads, cast by the lines of streetlights along the main with all the stores, the mall, and the Sunrise Sprinkles —*one, two, three, four*—I count. When I get to twenty-three lights, I hear the click of the door lock, and my mother enters.

"You'll never believe what happened," she says.

She is carrying another cardboard coffee cup from the lobby, a red lipstick print stamped on the plastic cover.

I'm still angry at her. Angry that I'm not sitting by the lake at my father's house because we're on this ridiculous trip. Angry that we're in Maryland, not Pennsylvania. And angry that she made me worry.

But there's a rush of relief. I hug her and she's shaking. I turn off the TV and she sits down on the bed, sighing softly as she drinks her coffee.

"It was so quiet when I walked in," she starts. "All the lights were on, but there was no one at the counter. I called out, but no one answered. So I pulled up the countertop and—"

"Don't tell me you walked into the kitchen," I interrupt.

"Well, of course I did. Why wouldn't I?"

She shakes her head.

"That poor woman. The look on her face. I knew she was gone, there was so much blood on the floor."

"Didn't you think for a minute that the person who attacked her could still be there?" I ask.

"I didn't," she says. "I was surprisingly calm. I just picked up the phone hanging on the wall and called 911. They were at the door in less than five minutes."

Mom was pleased that she remembered to tell the police the two inside areas that would have her fingerprints—the phone and the countertop.

"Must be my experience working for the newspaper," she says.

I don't remind her that she wrote about Spirit Week at school and Strawberry Festivals at the local church.

She answered all their questions but was sorry she couldn't provide much information. No—she didn't see anyone leaving when she arrived. No—she didn't notice anyone driving out of the parking lot.

With her contact information recorded, they let her leave. I'm sure they could tell my mother was crazy, but not stab a Sunrise Sprinkles employee kind of crazy. Although sometimes I wondered if my mother was even crazier than anyone knew.

Chapter 5

I awake to the smell of burnt coffee, as she carries two cardboard cups from the lobby and places one on the bedside table.

"Green tea," she says. "They had hot water in the lobby, but no tea of any kind. The woman at the desk scouted around and came back with a tea bag for you."

"Thanks," I say, sitting up in bed. "Do they have food downstairs? I'm hungry."

"No food downstairs, but the Bagels and Grinds place is just down the road."

I take a few sips, then pull the top items from my suitcase—a pair of blue gym shorts and a white t-shirt imprinted with "Surf" and a squiggly line that resembles a wave. I slip on my neon green flip flops and we're out the door. Nothing makes me move faster than hunger.

On our drive, we pass the Sunrise Sprinkles. Three police cars are parked at the curb with two news crews on the upper section of the parking lot. My mother takes a long look as we sit at the light.

"That poor woman. I can't stop thinking about her face."

The scene is different at Bagels and Grinds. We walk by a courtyard fountain with blue lights highlighting the rising water and pass the outdoor tables where a large family is laughing and dropping pieces of their breakfast on the pavement for their golden retriever.

Just inside the entrance, there's a glass-enclosed area with large stainless-steel fixtures, which a sign identifies as a water treatment facility that produces three types of ultra-purified water. Wow—that's taking coffee making to a whole new level.

My mother is already at the counter looking over the bagels in the display case. With her index finger resting on her lips, I notice her nail and lip colors are a near-perfect match.

"Could I do an egg sandwich on a bagel?" she asks.

"Of course you can," says the man behind the counter with short, mostly gray hair and glasses, whose nametag reads "Stan." "Do you want some melted cheese on that—provolone, mozzarella, cheddar?"

"Why not—let's do provolone," she says. "Anna Lee?"

I order the Eggstremely Healthy Breakfast—egg white, baby spinach, and chipotle mayo.

"Have a seat and I'll deliver it to you when it's ready," says Stan.

I find a table by the window while Mom reads all the coffee urn labels on the beverage counter. She reads the labels a second time before making a choice.

The side window faces a street, but there's another outdoor dining area with small trees lit by full morning sun. A guy and girl about my age sit at one of the tables, both with eyes fixated on phones, switching between smiles and scowls as they scroll. I wonder if their mothers would force them to travel to the wrong Hanover in a crazy quest for coffee.

Mom returns to the counter and talks with Stan. I notice her hand touch his as they laugh about something he says. I can't hear the whole conversation, but she mentions the Costa Rican coffee she's drinking, and her voice rises on words like *robust* and *zest*. "All free-trade coffee," he says. Stan has another coffee cup in his hand and they're walking toward the bins where he's describing the Jamaican blend he'd like her to try.

I pull out my phone to do some mindless scrolling. I'm still disappointed no one has sent me a text. Not even a response from last night. I bet if I tell them about the murder and my mother's role they'll respond. Although that's just more evidence that my mother is crazy. And I'm the daughter of a crazy woman. No wonder it's hard for me to make friends. Most of my friends are either back in high school or have started college—they're too busy to even notice I'm gone.

I finished high school a year early so my parents expected me to start college this fall. My mother and I made the trek to several schools for tours and information sessions. I'm not surprised I don't get into my top choice, Stanford. My SAT scores were strong, but not strong enough. When I talked to my guidance counselor, she agreed it was a stretch application, but I should work toward my goal. I didn't tell her it was my goal primarily because of its distance from New Jersey.

I did get acceptance letters from University of Maryland, Penn State, and University of Delaware, but dragged my feet and missed the deadlines to commit. I told my mother I'd miss her too much, and she believed me. So when I suggested staying home while she traveled alone, she used my own words against me.

"But Anna Lee—you'll miss me too much!"

Staying with my father was out for the same reason. Whether my mother knew all along that missing her was just an excuse to delay the start of college, I don't know. Lessoned learned–I better be careful about my excuses in the future.

She is back at the table now and Stan is putting down our plates. I already have my fork and knife in my hands and am eating my first bites as they continue their conversation.

"It's just tragic," he says. "I know a few detectives in the county police department and they stopped in this morning."

Mom must have told him about her discovery.

"They're already leaning toward the husband," he says. "Got an APB out on him. I sure hope they find him soon. If he's not the one who did it, they need to rule him out and keep searching."

I'm still eating as they talk. By the time I've finished my Eggstremely Healthy Breakfast I have all the facts on the case. The victim and her husband were the only two employees working the last shift—a time typically low on customers. They were on work visas from India and lived in the apartments behind the Sunrise Sprinkles. The first stop police made was to the apartment. They found the wife's passport in the top, unlocked drawer of a small desk, along with other important papers, but the husband's passport was not there. Stan must have some tight connections with the police. I always thought they kept that information close hold until the case played out.

"I'll let you enjoy your breakfast," Stan says. Looking at me, he adds, "Looks like you've already enjoyed it! Can I get you anything else?"

I'm chewing my last bite, but I give him a closed-mouth smile as I shake my head.

I watch her eat the egg sandwich, her red lipstick fading with each bite. The small restaurant is less crowded now, most people walking out with a cup of coffee and a small bag in hand. For normal people, the morning cup of coffee is a way to kick start the day—then it's on to the main attraction. For my mother, coffee *is* the main attraction.

Stan is walking back toward us.

"Here's my contact info," he says, placing a business card in front of her on the table. "If you have any questions about coffee or just want to keep in touch, I wrote my cell on the back. I'd love to hear about your journey."

Mom holds the card to her chest.

"I've found a kindred spirit," she says and they both laugh. "A coffee spirit! Nice to meet you Stan!"

I wonder if Stan drinks 10 cups of coffee a day or if he drinks none. I'm thinking it's closer to none. Smelling coffee, making coffee, serving coffee—it all must be too much. I bet Stan's not a kindred spirit at all. His coffee is all about money.

My mother's phone is ringing, an actual old-fashioned ringing phone sound that I find annoying. After last night, I guess she decided to keep her phone turned on.

"Oh! It's your father," she says, picking up the phone and moving toward the door in one movement. "Well hello there…" Her voice is pleasant, almost breezy as she steps outside the door and onto the sunny patio, which is empty now.

Despite the disaster at my father's only wedding, my parents are civil. They are neither friends nor enemies. Their relationship floats comfortably in the space between the two, at least most of the time. They had multiple conversations while my mother planned our trip—maybe my father was pleading for me to stay with him. Outside, she looks serious, then she nods her head vigorously and laughs before ending the call. Before I have a chance to come up with a reasonable explanation for my mother actually laughing when talking with my father, she's back at the table.

"Well, your father can't believe we went to the wrong state," she says, still laughing. "He told me that was vintage Jackie!"

No one called her Jackie, except my father. She introduced herself as Jacqueline, and when someone slipped a friendly "Jackie" into the conversation, she immediately corrected them.

"Did you tell him you found a dead body?" I ask.

"That poor woman! Don't speak about her that way!"

"What way? She was dead, right?"

My mother just shakes her head and pulls her enormous red purse to her shoulder.

"Goodbye, Stan," she calls out with a wave. "I'll be in touch!"

His whole face brightens, and I half expect him to blow her a kiss.

On the way back to the hotel, we pass Sunrise Sprinkles again. The police cars and news crews are still there. The "Open" sign is dark and there's not a single car in the drive-thru lane. A bright purple and pink sign with flags announces: *Happy Hour! Hot and iced coffee 50% off 2-6 p.m.* Because normal people don't drink coffee that late in the day.

My mother refilled her cup at Bagels and Grinds before we left, so she doesn't stop by the complimentary coffee pots in the lobby. She pulls out a few brochures from the rack next to the desk before we head back to the room.

"What do you think, Anna Lee? They have a horse show and dinner at the Mall.

Remember that time you rode the pony at Cindy's birthday party?"

I don't correct her.

"There's an indoor ice rink nearby and miniature golf. Or maybe we could get our nails done. Think about what you'd like to do this afternoon, and I'll freshen up."

I check my phone again—no messages from my friends. I unzip my luggage, reach in and pull out my *100 reasons why my mother is crazy journal.* I feel slightly guilty, but I turn the page and write: *#2 - Found a dead body at the Sunrise Sprinkles.*

Chapter 6

When I was 10, the city of Northern Beach started curbside recycling. The earth-conscious residents of the town no longer had to separate their plastic and paper and tin, then drive it to the large white bins near the library.

My mother covered the story for the Gazette, posted the list of recyclable items on our fridge, and dragged the large yellow bin to the curb each week. Until her nail snagged on the corner of the plastic. Then the responsibility of helping the environment was passed to me.

On the first night of my duty, I discovered a secret. As I pulled the heavy square bin behind me, I heard the sound of rolling, then glass clinking beneath the flattened cereal boxes and newspapers. At the end of our two-car-length driveway at the curb beside the mailbox, the streetlight and crescent moon were just bright enough. I moved the cardboard and paper back to see what made the sound. Wine bottles. A dozen or more. Maybe my mother had saved them up, I'd reasoned. Maybe she'd planned to do something with them and had them stashed away. I never saw her drink wine, although occasionally, I'd see a wine glass in the sink or drying on the towel on the countertop.

The next week, I figured the bin would be lighter. But it wasn't. Each week at the mailbox, I'd get a sick feeling in my stomach as I pulled back the stuff on top. And there they were. Fifteen, sixteen, seventeen wine bottles. The most was twenty-two. I turned them over to read the labels: Pino Noir and Pino Grigio. Sauvignon Blanc, and Cabernet Sauvignon. And lots of Sangria. The yellow price stickers revealed my mother's top criteria for her selections—nothing over $10.

Week after week, I'd drag that bright yellow bin to the curb, the bottles rolling around like bowling pins that had been knocked down.

After about a year of recycle duty, my mother had surgery and I stayed with my father. But when I returned, recycle duty was easier. As I started to drag the bin, my left foot caught and I almost lost my balance. I had pulled hard, but the bin was lighter. Much lighter. At the curb I saw why. Under the paper and cardboard were cans of corn and kidney beans, which my mother used that week to make her version of chili con carne.

And I noticed other changes.

My mother planted a garden. Not just a small one, either. She worked on that garden nearly every evening in the spring, pulling up grass, adding more dirt, planting clippings and bulbs from her friends' flower beds, and even digging up day lilies in the woods. She bought two red rose bushes at the Farmer's Coop, and I bought her a new one for Mother's Day with miniature pink roses. She liked it so much that rose bushes became my annual present. Eventually, the garden bordered our whole house, with the exception of the front and back doors. She spent a lot of time out there—weeding, thinning plants, and pruning bushes. It was almost an obsession, although not as all-consuming as coffee.

She also became obsessive about church—on one night especially. Every Wednesday night, even though I protested that I was old enough to be home alone, her friend Edna watched me so my mother could attend her *church meeting.* We'd never attended church, with the exception of Christmas Eve services. But about six months into her *church meetings,* we became regulars at the local Methodist Church. A few people seemed to know my mother, so at the time, I thought she must have been on some church committee that met on Wednesday nights. She read the Bible each morning while drinking her morning coffee and started posting scripture verses on post-it notes that she left around the house. On the bathroom mirror, on the fridge, even outside on the windows over her garden. There was one that reappeared regularly: *Therefore if any man be in Christ, he is a new creature.*

Once a month, Calvary Methodist hosted a donut social in the hall after services. My mother headed straight for the large stainless-steel coffee pot. At the table, she would warm her hand on the sides of the Styrofoam cup, then raise it to her red lips, pausing slightly before she closed her eyes and tilted her head back. It reminded me of the religious rituals during our service—especially on Communion Sunday.

Here, in the wrong Hanover, my mother practices her ritual again. She's just topped off her coffee at the hotel, warming her hands, raising the cup, reverently closing her eyes, tilting back her head.

Chapter 7

Before we head to our next location, we make one more stop—Baltimore-Washington Coffee Company. I'm an instant fan. Coconut iced coffee, which I sip slowly outside on the enormous wood deck. Laughter from the nearby childcare center lifts over the building.

I'm still thinking about those happy kids, wondering what it would be like to be so carefree when we start our drive. The windows are down and the music blaring. Bachman Turner Overdrive. Or maybe The Guess Who. My mother's braids whip around like a flag in gale-force winds as she sings to match the volume of the music, thrusting her chin in and out to match the beat of the song. Definitely Bachman Turner Overdrive.

The landscape transitions slowly from identical houses on identical streets to identical cows and horses grazing in identical fields. I remember those images of our original destination and my mouth is suddenly salty.

"Are we going to the *real* Hanover?" I ask.

My mother laughs. "That's in the past, Anna Lee!"

I wonder how a place could be in the past when we've never been there.

"So, where *are* we going? Do you even know?"

"Of course I know where we're going! Stan told me about another good spot in Maryland, near a big lake."

I roll my eyes back, thinking of our last trip to a beach without a plan. She and her friends were big fans of the *Housewives of New York* reality show. One night after watching the show, she decided we'd take a trip later that week to the Hamptons. When I asked about hotel reservations, she assured me the women on the show frequently and spontaneously visited the Hamptons.

We drove five hours. At some points, we inched along behind huge tractor trailers, my only view–the "how's my driving" sticker with a 1-800 number, the sour scent of the city mixing with the thick exhaust fumes. My mother tried to compensate by singing along with The Beach Boys.

When we arrived, she found out that other people did have a plan when they went to the Hamptons. They had to. There wasn't a single place with a vacancy—at least within our budget. There were two hotels with open suites, but we left after seeing the rate. I learned later those reality show ladies could make a last-minute decision—because they owned houses there.

After spending the first two hours driving to the rental agencies, hotels, and bed and breakfasts, she decided we'd spend the rest of our day doing everything on our itinerary. The activities we'd originally planned for a weekend were now compressed to a frenzied eight hours.

We tried on clothes at expensive boutiques but didn't buy any. We sampled enough high-end fudge and ice cream to leave us satisfied, for free. We walked through a craft fair, where my mother tried on two necklaces. The artists looked hopeful, but in the end she walked away. We spread our blue and white mock-quilt blanket on a quiet section of the beach, and unpacked the small red cooler with a homemade, recreated menu she saw on the show: chicken salad sandwiches on croissants, pasta salad, melon wedges, and a glass container of raspberry iced tea. Later, we shook off the sand and spread our blanket over the uniformly green grass in a nearby park for a free concert. I took off my sandals and stretched out my legs, listening to a woman not much older than me with shiny, long black hair singing Jewel, Alanis Morrissette, and some other artists I'd never heard.

We did spend some money. She recognized the coffee shop the teenaged daughters in the show visited. We sat outside at a small round table on chairs with striped green padded seats. We sipped cappuccino (hers) and chai tea (mine), watching families that resembled the people on the show walk by. From my mother's account, we "people watched." From my account, the people watched her. Although she uncharacteristically wore a toned-down outfit, a peasant styled top and long skirt—both white–I didn't see any other women with tiny blonde braids in their hair.

That evening, we spent the most money. My mother carefully reviewed menus outside restaurants. After realizing she couldn't afford places featured on the show, she settled on a cozy Italian place where we split a pizza.

At 10 p.m., we started the long drive home. The roads were less crowded but only lit by streetlights and the mere shadow of a moon hidden behind clouds. I felt myself dozing off every few minutes, my head dropping each time and startling me awake.

"Are you okay, Mom?" I would ask, before falling back asleep again.

Of course, my mother's frequent stops for coffee infused enough caffeine into her bloodstream to keep her awake for the drive. We pulled in front of the house a little before 2 a.m.

So here we are now, flying down Route 70 in our rusted red Jeep, with only a recommendation from Stan the stranger. I wonder if we'll ever make it out of Maryland. My only consolation is the mention of a lake. Maybe I'll find an Adirondack chair and pretend I'm at my father's—assuming we actually find a place to stay for the night.

Eventually, my ears start to clog. The view turns from barns with peeling, sun-faded red paint and fields of brown and gold stalks, to walls of pitted, glittering gold and tan rock, where the road cuts directly through the mountain.

I see the first billboard and I'm looking for more. We drive another mile and there's one for a restaurant (*We only serve Angus Beef!*) and another for a hotel right after (*Seventh Night Free!*). We must be close. We drive over a bridge where I see the lake. It looks like an ocean compared to the lake behind my father's house.

The first two small hotels we pass have "no vacancy" signs. My already low expectations drop.

"Did Stan mention the places here are usually booked in advance?" I ask.

My mother remains fixed on the road, but turns anxiously whenever we near another building that looks like potential lodging. Luck is on her side. At the next place the "no" is unlit.

Willow at the Lake isn't a chain hotel, but it's not an aging motel either. It fits with the scenery of the surrounding mountains, and when we step into the small lobby, I can see a wide view of Deep Creek Lake out the back windows. After checking in, we pass a large indoor pool and hot tub on the way to our room.

"Let's visit the pool after we check out Stan's suggestion," my mother says.

With no familiar coffee scent in the lobby, I'm not surprised we'll be making a straight shot for caffeine. But just inside the room is a small coffeemaker.

"You know what? I think we can check the pool out first," she says, pretending that her newfound access to coffee doesn't have anything to do with the change in plans.

"I didn't bring my swimsuit," I say.

"I thought you might forget, so I packed one for you!"

I didn't forget, but decided it wasn't worth the energy to argue. And the last time I argued with her, she almost wound up on the floor of Sunrise Sprinkles, surrounded by pink and purple frosted donuts and the scents of coffee. Although, drifting off in that atmosphere would likely be her idea of heaven.

My mother packed the swimsuit I hate. It's bright teal, and as I scrunch up my nose, my mother assures me "that's your color, Anna Lee!" The color is beside the point. It's a two-piece with boy-shorts. My belly curves over the waist band.

I change, throw on a t-shirt imprinted with a palm tree that has five lush branches (another purchase not made by me) and wait on the balcony until she finishes her coffee and gets ready. The wobbly plastic Adirondack chair isn't as comfortable as the wood version at my father's house.

The floating dock for *Willow at the Lake guests only* dips down and up as a lone jet ski unsettles the water. In the distance, I see two pontoon boats moving so slowly I mistakenly think they've dropped anchor.

The mountains surrounding the lake are dotted with a few colors: orange, red, muted purple, yellow-gold. It's early fall, so most trees still cling to their green leaves. Five colors, plus a medium blue sky above. The reflection on the lake is not a series of colors, but a single, dazzling unknown color.

In addition to my obsession with counting, I have a fixation with color. I see differences in shade that others don't notice. My mother claims it as my gift, but she's wrong. It's a curse.

Most people think hues are close enough, like those nearly-matched red tones in my mother's outfits. Pillows and furniture designed to blend with walls, billboards, television advertisements, magazine covers—most of the color associations are *off*.

My mother also claims my writing skills as a gift. I do like to write, although I'd never admit that to my mother. I even had a couple of my short stories published in our school literary magazine over the last year. Another piece of information I'll never share with her. And if I were to become a full-time writer, my mother would immediately claim me as her mini-me. Yeah, that's not going to happen. Maybe I could write under an alias. What would my name be? Initials so my gender isn't used against me? In my gender studies class, our teacher mentioned it's been historically easier for men to get published.

The scent of the room-brewed coffee finally reaches the balcony when I hear her voice.

"Ready for the pool?"

Chapter 8

The pool is big. So big that no matter how energetic the kids in the shallow side grow, I can exist in a giant splash-free zone. Their laughter and calls of "Marco Polo" echo off the white walls and tiled floors.

I dive in and surface quickly, resting the back of my head on the water and reaching behind me to pull the cool water toward my body as I breathe in chlorine. Right arm, left arm in and repeat as I stare up. There's a small section in the center of the ceiling that's patched—the white paint almost matching. With my ears floating just below the surface, all sound muffles. I concentrate on my hands, slightly cupped as they raise and release the water, a gentle, consistent rhythm forming until I start to forget about this trip.

I swim faster, touch the edge with stretched fingertips, execute a precise flip turn to rise again. At our community pool in the summer, the swim coach always praises my flip turns. Truth is, I don't like to stay beneath the surface, so I've perfected the speed of my turns to return to the surface quickly. I also hate to rest my face on top the water. The backstroke is my favorite.

There's something soothing yet terrifying about water. In the warm weather at my father's lake house, I'd walk out a few yards in the shallow water, holding a beach towel and a book over my head until I reached the wood platform he'd installed at my urging. Actually, he'd paid to have installed—he wasn't even there to watch the progress.

I'd lay out on that platform for hours, the steady rhythm of the water barely moving the platform. How many books had I read in the middle of the lake? I'd never stopped to count, but I do remember a few from last summer, when I decided to only read books on my wooden island with the word *water* in the title: "The Color of Water," "The Water is Wide," "Water for Elephants," "Like Water for Chocolate," "Night Over Water." Turns out, there were more books than I expected. I'd already read Sylvia Plath's "Crossing the Water" in school but decided to it read again during my summer of water.

My mother seemed to understand my obsession with books, although she was strictly a nonfiction reader. I wish all those self-help books she read came with a guarantee. My father didn't read at all. He said the last book he'd read was in school. Because he *had* to.

"Now I don't have to read them, so I don't," he said. "When you finish school, you won't have to read them either."

It would take too much energy to explain why I loved to read and my father probably wouldn't understand anyway.

One of my other favorite places to read was by the ocean, exactly five blocks from my mother's house. The sound of the waves was a soothing, white noise backdrop, although I kept my distance from the edge of the water. The ocean is unpredictable; the lake soothing.

I look up to see if my mother is still on the chair. She's there, shaking her coffee cup which is probably empty. And she's staring straight at me.

She smiles. "How's the water? Warm enough?"

"Not bad. I bet the hot tub feels even better. Wanna join me?"

She rises so quickly from the chair she must be afraid I'll change my mind.

I follow her, and as I sink into the warm, foamy water, I close my eyes for a moment. The loud push of the bubbles makes conversation nearly impossible, but my mother is trying.

"Do you want…"

"What?"

"We could…"

"What?"

"I thought we…"

"I can't hear you," I shout.

She smiles and tilts her head back on the tile, and I do the same. Maybe when we return to New Jersey, I could talk my father into buying a hot tub.

I remember how hungry I get after a swim. It's 3 p.m. before my mother is finally finished her shower and dressed. The last time we ate was breakfast.

"Does this place we're going to have food?"

"Stan said they have soups and sandwiches."

The drive along the lake is so absorbing, I almost forget about food. Two pontoon boats. Three small fishing boats. Six kayaks. Ten piers. But as we pull into the parking lot at Trader's Coffee House I can already smell the food before we get out of the Jeep.

After I order a spinach pesto quesadilla, I sit at one of the open tables and look around. It would take hours to count the coffee mugs for sale in the large wooden display case. Same with the signs, which are scattered everywhere.

Relax You're at the Lake
The Lake is Calling

The Mountains are Calling
Got Coffee?
The Best Coffee in Town
Just Give Me the Coffee and No One Gets Hurt

There are multiple chalkboards as well, with practical information like the list of smoothies or lunch specials. The writing is perfectly executed with the precision of an artist, or a teacher with years of practice at the blackboard. I wonder if someone has to change those boards each day.

There is so much to look at in this place—muffins and cookies in a glass display case, bags of coffee beans, boxes of specialty teas, glass jars filled with biscotti. And there is some-thing else–bottles of wine. I glance at my mother and she's looking straight at them, pursing her lips together like she does when she's annoyed.

Fortunately, our lunch–and my mother's coffee–arrives quickly, and her focus shifts from the wine racks to her plate.

Stan was right about the food. The quesadilla is so good I will myself to slow down, to enjoy despite my hunger. I'm not completely successful.

"Let's get something sweet and sit by the fire," my mother says.

A raspberry-flavored iced tea and chocolate-chip scone for me and a coffee refill and biscotti for my mother. She starts to sit on the sofa, then moves closer to a chair by the stone fireplace. Is she looking for warmth, or does she choose this seat so the wine bottles will be out of view?

"Did I ever tell you about the time you went skiing?" she asks.

"Me? I don't remember!"

"It would be quite a surprise if you did remember!" she laughs. "Your father took me for a weekend in the Poconos.

We had a great time skiing and even went horseback riding on a snow-covered mountain."

I tried to imagine some magical world where my parents did fun stuff. Together.

"When we arrived home, I started to feel sick to my stomach, even thought it could be something related to the recent altitude change. Didn't take me long to find out I was pretty early in my pregnancy. So technically, you went skiing!"

"My first and last ski trip. Too bad I'll never remember it!"

My mother tilts her head to the side and closes her eyes briefly.

"We stayed in a small cabin by the slopes," she says. "It looked so cozy, the kind of place you'd expect in the mountains. But when we stepped inside, it was freezing. Your father jiggled the thermostat, but it wouldn't kick on. I thought he'd get angry, but he kept repeating, 'the best laid plans...'"

I laugh, "I've heard that phrase before!"

My father is comfortable with structure. Rigid, unchanging structure. He loves the expected. Unlike my mother.

"So, what did you do?" I ask.

"We went back to the car and your father turned on the ignition and started the heater. He told me to stay in the car— he had a plan."

"He always has a plan!"

"There was a stash of firewood under a big plastic tarp. He cleared off one section of snow, pulled the tarp back and carried an armful of firewood into the house. All I kept thinking was—I hope he finds some matches," she says. "It wasn't too long before he was back to turn off the car. It was still cold inside, but we placed the pillows from the sofa on the hearth so we could sit close to the fire, which was really putting out some heat. He grabbed the quilt off the bed and folded it over me."

She smiles. My mother generally didn't smile or even look pleasant when she mentioned my father. This story is contrary to what I imagine about my parents' relationship. They aren't hostile, but there's an occasional mumbling of words like *clueless* and *crazy*.

"Just as the place warmed up enough for us to take off our coats, we heard a loud, metallic thump. The heater finally started. After an hour with the fireplace going and the heat at full blast, we were sweating. We had to take a walk in the woods to cool off," my mother shakes her head and laughs. "Your father never had to start another fire. The heat stayed on at the highest setting all weekend—it never cycled off. Made it easy to get up in the morning and head out to the coolness of the slopes!"

"I didn't realize either one of you skied. Why did you stop?"

She looks down. "I guess that was more of your father's thing." she says. "Want to take a drive up to see the ski resort? I think it's nearby."

She steps up to the counter and asks the lady who took our order for directions.

"It's super easy," she says. "Make a left out of the parking lot and follow the signs."

Super easy for most people. She didn't know my mother.

Chapter 9

As described, the quick trip to Wisp Resort is well-marked with signs. And as I expect, my mother still gets lost. We are in a residential area of narrow, curving roads. At least every third house is marked by an *available for rent* sign with one of two local leasing company names. The signs also include phrases like *lake view, direct lakefront, view of slopes, hot tub*, and even an occasional *heated pool*.

"Which one would you pick if you could?" I ask.

My mother settles on a simple log cabin up on the hill with *lake view*. I pick a stone ranch home that is *direct lakefront*, until I see a similar design that promises both *direct lakefront* and *hot tub*.

In the distance, we spot a sign for Wisp and follow it up a winding road to the entrance. A group of young, tanned guys all in light purple polo shirts, probably branded with the landscaping company's name, are lifting shovels of mulch from the back of a pick-up truck and spreading it over the flower bed that's filled with crimson and gold mums.

We park in the nearly empty lot and walk into the lodge. Floor-to-ceiling windows extend to a cathedral-height wood ceiling, the building perfectly positioned to view the slopes. I imagine it a few months from now—white, crystalized snow light on the trails, heavy on the pine trees, the white evolving into new colors under the sun. I focus on the hills, hoping to materialize my parents skiing down the slope. Not my parents *now*; my parents *then*.

"Are you checking in?"

My mother steps toward the desk.

"We're staying nearby. Thought we'd visit this lovely resort," she said, sweeping her arms around.

The dark-haired woman with glasses behind the front desk is putting together brochures.

"Maybe the next time you're in the area, you'll stay with us," she says. "Here's some information on our packages and amenities. Take your time, look around."

"Anywhere I can get a refill?" my mother asks, shaking her cardboard cup with the coffee shop logo.

"Well, it's not as refined as Trader's coffee," she says quietly, like she doesn't want her unseen supervisor to hear. "But, please help yourself."

She motions toward two coffee pumps. My mother turns so quickly that she leaves the brochures on the counter.

"Don't forget these," the woman says. "And you might consider our mountain coaster."

My eyebrows involuntarily rise. A mountain coaster? It's certainly something I'd like to consider, but I'm not sure my mother would. When I was younger, she encouraged me to be adventurous. In recent years, she squelched any slightly exciting activity I suggested—rock wall climbing, water skiing, whitewater rafting. A mountain coaster. She'll never do it. I'm looking at the slopes again when she responds.

"Where do we catch it?"

Until I'm seated on the mountain coaster, I expect she'll change her mind.

"I'm right behind you, Anna Lee," she says, sliding behind me, her legs touching mine.

The attendant laughs, "She'll be fine. No one has fallen off the mountain yet, and today's not going to be the day."

He reviews the safety instructions. The ride starts slowly, the wind crisp against my face. This must be how skiing feels. Maybe a part of my brain still held that feeling from my earliest moments, before my parents even knew I existed. Independence, weightlessness, freedom. I feel them all so strongly that I start to laugh. My mother is laughing too. There's a slow glide near the bottom, then a hard stop. As I exit and look back, the same joy I feel is replicated on my mother's face. Is she thinking of that ski trip with my father? Before Miss June? Before me?

She jumps out and hugs me tightly.

"Let's do it again, Anna Lee!"

We ride the mountain coaster two more times.

When we return once again, the attendant smiles.

"I'm thinking you two ladies enjoyed this ride more than anyone I've ever seen, and I've seen a lot," he says. And he gives us a fourth ride for free.

The sun is just starting to ease closer to the lake on our drive back to Willow. She doesn't turn the radio up and she doesn't talk. As a bonus, we make it back to the main road without getting lost.

Almost impulsively, my mother turns the wheel sharply into the parking lot of Trader's Coffee House.

"Just stay here—I'll only be a minute," she says.

She trips slightly on the curb and pulls the door so hard it almost hits her in the face. It's been a couple of hours since she finished her last cup. I wonder if she's feeling lightheaded, like a diabetic who needs a quick hit of sugar.

There's a menu for the pizza place on the second floor posted on the building. Good selection and they even have one with crab and veggies. I'm still reviewing when I hear a bang. My mother pushed out of the door so hard she hit the cement wall.

She's gripping a large cardboard cup with the Trader's brand on the sleeve in her hand, and she stops to take a sip. That's when I notice something else. Something that makes my stomach feel unsettled, and it's not from the mountain coaster.

Her red, soft leather purse has a bulge on the side, and I know the shape well—it's a wine bottle.

Chapter 10

The remains of the sun rest unevenly on the lake—bright reflections side-by-side with pockets of darkness where clouds cover the light. Gone is the feeling of independence I felt on the coast. It's replaced by an old, familiar question that lives within me. When will my mother start drinking again?

The air feels cool on the balcony and my mother warms her hands around her Trader's coffee cup.

"Are you cold?" she asks.

I want to ask what's in her purse. I want to ask if memories of her time on the mountain with my father set her back. I want to ask if spending time with me isn't enough. Isn't enough to keep her from failing. Instead, I just shake my head.

My mother doesn't know I remember. The recycle bin. Those water glasses rimmed with red at the bottom. Evening "quiet" time in her room while I watched TV alone. She doesn't know I remember her curses when she banged her foot against walls and furniture. She doesn't know I remember the night she forgot to shut off the oven—the cookies permanently fused with the baking sheet, the smoke waking me. She doesn't know that I only invited friends to visit early. Never after dinner.

And there's something she'll never know unless I tell her. The time she passed out on the couch and I got lost in the neighborhood. Sometimes I tell myself it never happened. Childhood imagination. Except it wasn't. That memory was the reason I tried not to argue with my mother. Why I didn't forget to pick up my room and do my laundry. Why I didn't ask for too much.

That night while she sleeps, I think about the bottle of wine in her purse. But no matter how much I want to confirm it's there, the desire to not know is stronger.

Eventually, I fall asleep and dream I'm skiing down a grass mountain. The air is warm—so warm that I'm wearing my swimsuit, my hair blowing left and right, mimicking my moves on the slopes. My parents are beside me, side by side, and we're moving together, laughing, happy. The pine trees are different shades of green, contrasting with different shades of grass. The sun warms the top of my head and I raise my face upward and close my eyes.

Suddenly my father is shouting and my eyes are open, staring straight ahead at the lake. We're moving too fast. My parents ski off to either side and I'm alone, the edge approaching, the water like black ink. Closer, closer until I catch on the edge of the grass, suspended for a moment before I fly into the water, turning over and over. Which way is up? I wiggle the skis off my feet and try to touch bottom. If I push off with all my strength I'll reach the top. But I can't find the bottom. With my eyes wide open, I spin to look for a crack in the surface where I can follow a single ray of the sun through the dark. But there is not even a sliver of light. I hold my hands out, stretching on my right and left to reach for my parents on either side. I'm alone.

Just as my head feels heavy and my body starts to sink, I feel a tiny vibration at my ear. The thinnest of voices, just loud enough to penetrate the thick darkness pressing in around me.

"Anna Lee! Anna Lee!"

I awake to the smell of coffee, mixed with something sweet. It's still slightly dark, but my mother is on my side of the room, wearing her pink polka-dot pajamas as she rocks back and forth waiting for the last drip.

"Are you ready to get up, sleepy head?" she calls over her shoulder. The machine seems to gasp a long exhale, then click off, and my mother takes a big gulp from her cup as she opens the shades and walks out on the balcony, her silk robe flowing behind her.

I step out of bed and see it. The bottle is right next to the coffee machine. What should I do? Grab it and wave it in her face? Empty the contents in the bathroom sink? Close my eyes until my mother realizes she left the evidence in view and removes it herself?

In a single motion I am out of bed, taking a step toward it, my heart beating fast. I see an Italian flag on the label, then read: *Torani Coconut Coffee Syrup.*

My next journal entry:

#3 She buys wine bottles filled with coffee flavoring.

Chapter 11

We have a plan, based on my mother's recent phone conversation with Stan. Our next stop will be St. Sabastian's Coffee in Alexandria, Virginia and then we'll drive another 3-1/2 hours to Virginia Beach.

Before my mother starts the engine, I gather up four empty cardboard coffee cups and three plastic lids from the floor and deposit in the trashcan at the end of the lot. There will be more by tomorrow, along with more coffee stains on the tan upholstered driver's seat. There's hardened brown sludge in the bottom of her cup holder. I'll need a wet cloth to clean that up later.

On the road, music fills the space between us, giving me some imaginary privacy. The record so far is 16 songs—just over an hour with no conversation. I share the ride with BB King, Bad Company, U2, and Chicago as we drive to Virginia. I try to count the different types of trees along the highway, but pine trees are tricky. There's a subtle difference between the short-needled ones and I'm quickly evaluating their structures.

She abruptly turns the music off.

"I'm sorry I never got you a dog," she says.

Most people need a reason to bring up a topic. Not my mother. We weren't talking about dogs earlier and there are no dogs within view.

"That's fine," I say flatly. "What made you think about a dog?"

She doesn't answer. As suddenly as the music stops, it's back on again. We were up to 12 songs before her dog statement. I wonder how many we'll get through this time.

This wasn't her first odd apology on our trip. We are just a few days in, and she has apologized that she didn't marry my father, give me a sister or brother, let me go camping with our neighbors. None of those things mattered to me. I couldn't imagine my parents spending every day together. My friends who had siblings were always complaining about them. And, I had no desire to sleep in a tent for a week. My mother's *no* gave me an easy excuse. I wondered if she'd apologize for something that did matter. Like never getting to meet her father–my grandfather.

I saw my father's parents once a year when they took the train down from Vermont. They sent me three cards a year with a $50 check in each for my birthday, Easter, and Christmas. They were quiet, almost shy people. My father and I took the train to visit them a few years ago when my Uncle Ben was in town. My dad's slightly older brother, he was divorced with no kids, lived in Northern California, and worked in the IT industry. I hoped he'd be a relative I could actually connect with, but he talked even less than the rest of the family.

My mother was an only child, and her parents were a mystery I was unable to solve, likely because I only had three facts: my grandmother died when my mother was a teen; my grandfather was still alive; and my mother refused to talk about them. And I only had my mother's word for all three facts. Occasionally, I'd work a question into our conversation, hoping to gather another fact or two: Were your mother or father a writer? Did your family go to the beach for vacation? What did your parents do for a living? Sometimes I was more obvious: How did your mother die? Where does your father live? Why don't you talk to him?

Every question resulted in the same terse response: "That's a closed subject."

Once, I asked my father.

"You know as much as I do," he said. "There are some subjects your mother won't discuss."

There was another question I never asked my mother, but I often wondered: does my grandfather know about me? I hoped the answer was no. What grandparent didn't want to meet their grandchild?

We are in the city now, navigating both cars and people carelessly crisscrossing intersections. I don't have my driver's license yet, but I do have my permit. When we left Deep Creek, I asked if I could drive to Alexandria.

"Let's wait 'til we're off the mountain roads," she said, but never pulled over to change seats. Thankfully.

The mountain roads would have been less stressful. Watching people jump out between cars with the same unexpected urgency of a jack-in-the-box makes me question ever driving in a city.

During the ride, I pull up images of St. Sabastian's. Now I see its prominent blue awning a couple streets away.

"Straight ahead, right up there," I say, pointing.

"Keep your eyes open for a parking spot," she says.

It isn't that easy. We drive a couple blocks past St. Sabastian's and circle twice before we see a car backing out from the curb. I squint in the bright sun to read the sign: St. Sabastian's Coffee *Pub.*

There's a sidewalk patio with umbrella-shaded tables.

"Alright if we sit outside?" I ask.

"Of course, Anna Lee. Let's see what's on the menu first."

Inside, there's a pleasant mix of paintings, photos, and sketches on the gold walls. The furniture is tightly spaced with square wood tables for four, a piano, and unmatched uphol-stered furniture in soft gold and blues. My mother is already chatting with the lady at the register.

The coffee bar runs across the side wall and has a similar chalkboard menu to Trader's—but the writing is less careful.

On the patio, the breeze breaks up the sun's cloudless heat. My iced mocha coffee is a logical drink for the weather, but my mother sips slowly as the steam from her cup merges into the warm air.

"That does look refreshing!" she says.

"Take a sip," I say, pushing it toward her.

She scrunches her nose but leans forward to take a slow sip through the straw. Her eyebrows raise.

"Oh! That's quite good—dessert-like," she says. "But I just can't get used to ice in my coffee. I guess I'm a purist!"

Laughter bursts out from me in a single HA, and she looks amused, then hurt. My mother's not a purist. She's not even particular about her hot coffee. Or her wine. I think about those bottles rolling around like lifeless, dirty white pins at the bowling alley. How many of those bottles were from the discounted shelf? White, red, Italian, French, local. Selections probably determined by price alone. Individually, they were cheap, but I didn't allow myself to calculate the collective cost.

"Can we take a vacation this summer?"

"Take tennis lessons?"

"Buy a new bicycle?"

"Go horseback riding?"

"Get a pizza for dinner?"

Her stock answer: "We can't afford it."

But she could afford wine—and lots of it. I wonder how my mother is funding this trip. Hotel stays, coffee shops, dinners, multiple rides on the mountain coaster. I struggle against my usual compulsion to count.

Growing up, I learned quickly that the path to any purchase required two stops. My mother was the first stop. My father was the second and final stop.

"Can I buy a new bicycle?"

"Ask your mother."

"I already did. She said we can't afford it."

With a heavy sigh as he opened his wallet, "How much?"

Sometimes I'd add another phrase, just to make the deal.

"All my friends are going horseback riding."

Or, buying new jeans, going to the movies, taking tennis lessons.

He never said, "We can't afford it."

My father owned a financial firm. Even when he wasn't at his office, his laptop was open and his eyes rarely strayed from the screen.

We didn't converse. He asked questions. I answered. He rarely listened to my responses.

"How was your day today?"

"Okay—I started a new book, one of the books you gave me for my birthday."

"Hmmm. What did you do?"

"Started a new book, one of the books you gave me for my birthday."

"A book? Did you ever read any of the books I gave you for your birthday?"

I never had to ask my father if we could order a pizza. Carryout was his go-to. Sometimes, after a typically late day, he'd swing by one of the delis near his office to pick up Italian cold-cuts. Other times, he'd arrive with still-hot Styrofoam containers of chicken parmesan from Mario's. Most often, he'd ask me to order delivery from Tony's Pizza and Subs. My father was Scottish, but he ate like an Italian.

The menu was limited, but at least I wasn't embarrassed to invite friends over. My mother's house was bright, with mismatched patterns—a reflection of her taste in clothes. The interior was painted gold, but each room, except my bedroom, had an accent wall—neon green in the kitchen, hot pink in my mother's bedroom, cherry in the living room. She'd strung flowered curtains purchased at yard sales between rooms, but tied them back. She described the look as a refined, New England style, until one of our neighbors looked around and asked, "Are you running some kind of brothel on the side?"

When friends visited my father's house for the first time, there was always a big reaction. I watched them when they arrived, their eyes wide, moving around the room—the professionally-decorated great room with plush leather furniture and the biggest flat screen on the market, the towering tray ceilings. The sunroom, with its matching coral-striped cushions on rattan furniture and floor to ceiling windows overlooking the lake. In the kitchen, the white Italian marble countertops that only held carryout containers, an oversized six-burner range that never held a simmering pot, a massive refrigerator with expired condiments and spoiling milk, and a double oven that never baked a tray of cookies. At least not since Miss June left.

"Your dad must be loaded! Are you rich?"

During those initial reactions by my friends, I smiled. But soon I remembered. This wasn't my house. I wasn't even a visitor like my friends. I was an inconvenience.

On one Saturday a few winters ago, he was already gone when I woke up. I finished off the cereal and milk for breakfast and ate cold leftover pizza from the night before for lunch. I finished one book and started another before I realized it was dark. My father still wasn't home, and I was hungry.

After the weekend, I told my mother, and her face tightened as she picked up her phone and walked into her bedroom, closing the thin door behind her.

"That was the agreement," she said on the phone, stretching out the last word. "You signed a contract, remember? To at least spend a little time with her. One day during the week and alternate weekends. Do you want her to grow up without a father?"

Before that call, I felt sorry for my father.

"I got stuck at the office again," he'd say when he arrived home late.

After that, I knew. He wasn't stuck at the office. He was stuck with me.

Chapter 12

She looks at her watch with the thick red plastic band. "The music starts in four hours."

"We have a plan," I remind her. "Virginia Beach is next."

There's no hotel reservation nor any other reason we must arrive before dark, but at least there's a suggestion of a plan. And after today, it might be our last.

"Music would have been nice," she says, as she backs up to pull away from the curb. "Steph said the guy has been playing there for over three years, and he sounds just like Eric Clapton."

St. Sabastian's Coffee Pub has music some nights and tonight is one of them. But I don't want to hang out in a coffee shop for another four hours.

"That place is in the past," I say. "Let's look forward to Virginia Beach."

She laughs.

We're heading south on Route 95, the mid-day traffic thick and the sun now mostly hidden beneath an expanding, flat ribbon of blue-gray clouds.

My mother hits the button to advance one of the CDs she made on her laptop for the trip.

"He's here somewhere," she says, listening to the first notes, then skipping to the next song. "Ahhh," she says, sitting back and drumming on the steering wheel while the introduction plays. I'm convinced my mother has a mixed CD for every occasion. I'm also convinced we'll be listening to Eric Clapton the whole way to Virginia Beach.

She's still singing, but something in the lyric must have hit her. Her voice breaks a bit and she swats her hand at her eyes and cheek while she sniffs.

"What's wrong?" I ask.

"I'm just sentimental," she says, with an unnatural smile. She turns the music down. "Did I ever tell you I was a singer?"

I laugh. "You still sing—all the time."

Her stiff smile relaxes. "No—professionally. Well, if you count singing in The Hideaway or Junior's Lounge as professional," she says.

Those two bars, which had been sold a couple times over the years but still maintained their names, were frequent settings for crimes in the "Police Beat" section of the paper, usually for fights, but also for the occasional stabbing, and at least once for a shooting.

"You sang in bars?"

"A long time ago, Anna Lee," she says frowning, the soft lines on her forehead quickly wrinkling, like the surface cracks that form on the icy lake each winter.

"Were you in a band?"

"Not really—just two of us. My friend played guitar and we both sang."

"How often did you perform?"

"Hmmm, almost every weekend for maybe four or five years," she sighs. "I don't usually think about that time in my life."

"Why did you stop—was it because you had me?"

"I still performed after you were born, but not as often," she says.

Another secret. Although this one didn't seem surprising. It certainly wasn't out of character for my mother to seek attention.

"Did my father ever come to see you play?"

"That's actually how we met," she says, glancing at me, then back to the road. "He was with some friends from the office at The Hideaway one night. That's when he worked for a small firm in town, before he started his own company. He was there three weeks in a row before he finally put down his beer, walked through the haze of smoke and over to the corner where we played."

"I just can't picture him in a place like that."

I also couldn't picture my father socializing with friends, listening to music, and talking with a woman he didn't know.

"It was a long time ago, Anna Lee. He wasn't as focused on his work as he is now. People change."

I try to imagine my father in a bar, laughing with friends, smiling at my mother from across the room.

"What kind of music did you sing?"

"I've got a CD with some of the songs from our set list—can you pull it out for me? It's labeled J&J."

I look through the case and find it, pop out the current CD and press the new one in place. The guitar work sounds pretty basic, but the vocals are surprisingly on point.

I glance over to watch her sing with the music. The ice cracks on her forehead are gone, her chin tilted up as the sun hits her face all at once.

I'm feeling generous.

"You sound just like her!"

She starts laughing. "Linda Ronstadt? Hardly. She's tough to emulate. I suppose all the women I tried to copy in those days were beyond my talent—Stevie Nicks, Carole

King, Annie Wilson. Wow—I even tried to pull off Aretha Franklin—can you imagine?"

She shakes her head.

"I suppose I was more confident then. Or maybe unwilling to admit I had limits."

"You must have been better than you remember," I say. "Otherwise the bars wouldn't keep asking you to return."

"Well, the truth is, one of my friend's brothers was the bartender at The Hideaway."

"What about Junior's?"

"I'm guessing no one ever wanted to play at Junior's," she says. "We practically had to beg them to pay us. And it was never the full amount."

"Why'd you keep going back?"

"It wasn't really about the money."

"I bet it was fun playing with a friend for so long. Someone I know?"

She lets a full two lines of the song go by before she answers.

"Yes—it was June."

She said it. The name that was never said. Never said by either of us. Even my father never said her name. And any evidence of her existence in my father's house, was gone—like a bleached crime scene.

I missed Miss June for a long time. She was normal and kind, but she left me with two odd people. She wasn't my actual mother, but there were many times I wished she was. We shared the same love of books and the water. Unlike my father, she actually talked with me. And unlike my mother, she didn't embarrass me with her need for constant attention.

"That's the first time I've heard her name in a long time," I say.

"Do you ever think about her?"

I pause, wondering how to answer.

"It's okay," my mother says. "It's okay if you think about her. I think about her too. Actually, a lot lately."

"I try not to think about her," I say, and it's the truest answer I can give. I hope that's the end of our Miss June discussion, but it's not.

My mother turns down the music.

"Why not?"

How can I tell my mother I don't want to talk about her because she meant so much to me? She meant more to me than my mother or my father.

"You can tell me," she says quietly.

I negotiate the choices in my head, considering one, then pushing it aside until I find something appropriate to say.

"I thought she cared about me," I say slowly. "And then she was gone. I never heard from her again."

Miss June and I were always together when I spent the weekend at my father's–sitting by the lake in the Adirondack chairs, talking about a book we'd both read. Even though I was young, she always knew the kind of books I would like, not the "self-help" ones my mother insisted I read. I thought about Miss June when I sat by the lake or was alone in my father's house late at night or ate cold pizza for dinner. For a long time, I wondered if she thought about me. I didn't wonder anymore.

The music is still playing. Two voices. Miss June and my mother, Jacqueline. J&J. I knew they were friends, but I didn't know how close they were. Five years. Playing every weekend, and probably practicing during the week. No wonder my mother showed up at the wedding. It was still crazy, but I was starting to see what drove her to it. She must have felt so betrayed.

She turns up the volume, and I stare out the window without much to see except the roofs of houses peering over rough concrete walls designed to keep the road noise separate from backyard barbecues and bedtime stories. Who are the people in all those houses? I picture parents watching Saturday morning cartoons with their kids, helping with homework, baking Christmas cookies together.

She's turning the music down again.

"I have letters from June."

"When did she write you letters?"

"The letters weren't for me," she says. "They were for you."

"I don't remember any letters."

My mother was always filling my "special box"—an old computer box she'd covered in floral wrapping paper—with my drawings, papers from school, and cards she gave me on my birthday and Christmas. I never looked in the box, but she must have put some old notes from Miss June in there.

"You haven't read them," she says. "She left the first letter in my mailbox before she moved. And she sent others. I have them all."

"You kept them?" I ask slowly, "Were they addressed to you?"

My mother pulls her sunglasses out of her purse and pulls down the visor. The sun hasn't changed.

"They're your letters, Anna Lee. All yours."

"Doesn't sound like it," I snap. "Why do you have them if they're mine?"

She shakes her head. "That's not an easy question for me to answer."

"It really is an easy question. Maybe answering isn't easy. Did you read them?"

"No, I never read them, not a single letter. They're all still sealed, even the most recent one that came right before we left."

"But you kept them. Did you ever plan to give me the letters?

"I did...I always knew I would. The time never seemed right."

"And the time is right now?"

Her shoulders slumped as she dropped her head for a moment before looking straight ahead, her shoulders back.

"The time is absolutely right."

"Why wasn't the time right before?" I ask, the last word louder than I intend.

"I had no way of knowing what she wrote about. There may be some things in there you don't know, and I wanted a chance to tell you first."

Suddenly, I was one of the siblings in *The Lion, the Witch, and the Wardrobe*, at the doors separating the known from the unknown. And once I stepped through, the known would forever change.

"Is Miss June my real mother?" I ask, trying to keep the excitement out of my voice.

My mother laughs. "No—of course not."

I keep looking out the side window so she doesn't see the disappointment on my face. And the anger. If I'm too angry, she might not give me the letters. Worse, she might start drinking again.

"I'll tell you. When we get to Virginia Beach we'll sit and we'll talk and I'll tell you everything."

The music is back up again and I let my mind imagine my mother and Miss June at The Hideaway, singing together, the smoke around them, sealing them away from everyone, even from my father watching at the bar.

Chapter 13

"Will you find us a place to talk, Anna Lee?"

We're in Virginia Beach now, driving down Pacific Avenue, the town emerging like single, still image frames of a movie: ocean-hotel-ocean-hotel-ocean-hotel. Before the map on my phone loads, I see a sign, "Belvedere Coffee Shop."

We park on the street and circle to the front of the Belvedere Hotel and onto the oceanfront boardwalk.

"Let's get our coffee and sit out here," she says.

Inside, it's plain but bright, and my mother orders her standard and for me, a green tea. She doesn't chat with the lady at the counter.

On the boardwalk, my mother walks past a couple of benches until she finds one that faces the ocean.

She takes a long sip, then a second. She's looking straight ahead, across the stretch of sand that leads to the water's edge. The waves are moving in and out, slower than usual it seems, and that's the only sound until she speaks.

"It was June. It was always June."

I wait for more, but she doesn't continue.

"What does that even mean?"

"It was never me. Your father wasn't interested in me, not even on that first night. It was always June."

"I'm sure it was you at some point—at least at the beginning," I say.

"That's the thing, Anna Lee. It never was." Her voice is strained, like she's trying to pull weeds from her garden that have rooted deeply.

"I don't get it. Then why were you two together in the first place? Why wasn't he with Miss June?"

"He asked about her, right at the beginning. But I told him June was 'practically engaged' even though she had broken it off with her boyfriend. By the time he realized the truth, I was pretty far along in my pregnancy."

The waves are rolling in and out, a predictable, solid rhythm that seems familiar, but always with an underlying feeling of dread for me. I'm startled as a Frisbee drops on the beach just a few feet away. A guy about my age, with hair just a shade lighter than the sand, runs to retrieve it. He doesn't even glance in our direction.

"Why would you say that to him? You knew it wasn't true."

"Truth is, I was jealous of June. She was a better singer, a better person. People liked her more. And any time guys talked to us, they were there to talk to June, never me."

The last thing I wanted to do was sympathize with my mother, but I had a half-dozen friends who were like Miss June. They were funnier and smarter. They had better hair, noses, lips, bodies. People liked being around them.

"So once he found out, he left you for Miss June?"

"It wasn't that black and white, Anna Lee. Your father and I realized even before you were born that we weren't going to be together. I figured he'd be with someone, but I didn't think it would be my best friend."

I shook my head. "Why wouldn't it be her? It would have been her at the beginning if you hadn't screwed things up for them."

"I couldn't help how I felt then. I suppose I always knew the whole thing was my fault, but I still couldn't accept it. Until just recently."

The Frisbee whizzes through my view, the dark gray waves rolling in the background, leaving thick foam on the edge of the beach.

"Do you want to read the letters, Anna Lee?"

"You brought them?"

"I did."

"All of them?"

She nods.

"Let's check in somewhere and I'll get them out of my suitcase for you—give you some privacy."

"OK. Do we know where we're staying?"

She turns to look across the boardwalk.

"Well, the Belvedere Hotel seems nice. And we're already here."

We walk back to the car in silence, pull our luggage from the trunk and roll it up to the front entrance. Inside, my mother requests a room, her voice at half-volume. I look around the lobby—no complimentary coffee station.

In the elevator, she pushes the button to the sixth floor and breaks the long silence.

"I know it's a lot to process," she says.

We're pulling our luggage across the elevator track and down the teal carpet, around one corner before we reach our room. Inside, I immediately see what we have—an ocean view—and what we don't have—a coffee maker. My mother is in front of me, looking around the room, then walks past me to the bathroom. By her disappointed expression, she didn't find one there either. She probably doesn't notice the view.

I pull back the sheer curtains. The Frisbee players are gone, but the rhythmic beat of the waves against the sand continues.

"Here it is," she says, lifting a shoe box from her suitcase. "Should I give you some privacy?"

I nod.

"They're all in here," she says, handing it to me. "And they're in order. The first one's at the bottom."

She opens the door, then looks back.

"I'll see you in a couple hours."

The door clicks shut, and I move the desk chair to the side of the bed for a view of the ocean. I pull off the lid and lift the contents—all held together with two rubber bands. It feels heavy. I turn the stack over to start at the beginning. It's a letter with just my name on the front, no address. This must be the one Miss June slipped it into my mother's mailbox before she left for Arizona.

I stare at my name, Anna Lee, written carefully, with flourish. I still remember her handwriting. Previously a substitute teacher at our elementary school, she has the penmanship of someone who teaches cursive writing. The note paper has little ladybugs lined up in a single row across the top of the ivory paper.

Dear Anna Lee,

This is the most difficult letter I've ever written. I'm leaving your father. We both agree it's for the best, and it's been known for a long time. There is only one reason I have delayed the move. YOU.

You have a mother and a father who love you. And you have a stepmother who loves you too.

Each time I planned to leave your father, my love for you kept me in place. I was unhappy with my marriage. But with you, there was only pure joy.

For a time, I'll be staying with family in Arizona. As soon as I'm settled, I'll send you my address and phone number. Until we talk again, I only ask that you remember my leaving has nothing to do with you and is the only reason I have stayed for so long.
   I love you,
   Miss June

I read the letter again. Then go back and re-read, "a stepmother who loves you too" tracing my finger across the letters, feeling the slight texture left by the blue ink. Carefully, I trifold the letter and place it back in the envelope, noticing there's a single tiny ladybug in the triangle of the envelope's flap.

I put the first letter on the nightstand and slide the next from the stack. It feels warm in my hands. This time, the envelope has my first and last name, followed by my mother's address. There's a post office box in Arizona listed on the top left. The same tiny ladybug is on the envelope, and as I lift the first fold of the paper, I see a line of them across the top.

Dear Anna Lee,

I miss you and wish I could see you! I'm staying with my sister May at her little cottage in Arizona. There's no lake here, but there's a lovely little stream that runs through May's property.

She lives in Sedona, a magical place of huge red boulders. I see only red, but I'm certain you would see every hue embedded in the stone!

I hope you'll be able to visit me here. The landscape, the weather, the people—all are so different than New Jersey. Life is slower. May has encouraged me to take my time finding a job, and I've decided to get to know the area first. I'm reading and hiking and listening to live music in the local cafés.

I never told you, but I used to sing and play guitar. I still have my old acoustic and have started to play again.

My sister's number is on the bottom of this letter. You may need more time. I will let you make the first call.
I love you,
Miss June

I read the third letter, then the fourth. Miss June is working again as a substitute teacher and continuing to practice her music. She describes two books she has finished and asks me if I've read them. She wonders if we could start a "by phone book club." The fifth item in the stack is a Christmas card. Not one from a generic box, but one from a card store inscribed: *To someone who is special to me.* Inside is a gift card for the bookstore at the mall. I'm holding the plastic gift card and all I can think is that I never sent Miss June a Christmas card or thanked her for the present.

The next letter includes a picture of huge boulders. She's written on the back, *the red rocks of Sedona.* She's right—even in the picture I can see so much more than just red—streaks of rust, gold, orange, and a tinge of forest green.

After carefully adding that letter to the stack, I stand and stretch. My mother is sitting directly below on the same bench where we talked earlier. Her back is to me, but I can see the coffee cup as she raises it to take a sip.

I keep reading. There's a birthday card, with a gift card to another store at the mall that sells music. *Happy 10th Birthday, Anna Lee! I hope you find some music that you love!*

In one letter, she describes some of the students in the fourth-grade class where she's substituting for a teacher who just had a baby.

There's a boy named Billy who loves to play little jokes, even on me! Fortunately, he has a big heart and never does anything mean. One day I had a black skirt on. Before I arrived, he used the chalk-board eraser to layer chalk on my seat. I didn't see it on the light wood chair and sat down to prepare my work. When I stood up to write on the board, I heard the laughter behind me. One of the students in the first row immediately turned on Billy and told me about the joke. I thought it was pretty funny myself, and the chalk came right off with a wet cloth.

There's another student in the class named Hannah. She has the same pretty shade of hair as you, and she loves books, too!

In some ways it's such a nice, sweet reminder of you. In other ways, it makes me miss you even more. And oh, how I do miss you, Anna Lee!

At the bottom of every letter and card, the same phone number is written, in perfect block lettering that's even neater than the cursive writing on the page.

I stretch my neck for a longer view of the beach and see my mother on a different bench, one that faces the hotel. She's staring up toward the window.

I slide out the next letter in the stack, then adjust myself back in the chair so she's no longer in view.

Chapter 14

I've only read a quarter of the letters when there's a quiet knock at the door. I keep reading. There's a louder knock. I look up from the letter and wait.

"Anna Lee! I forgot my key."

I fold the letter, leave it on the chair, then walk half-speed to open the door. I turn quickly so I don't have to look at her.

"How's it going?" she asks tentatively.

I don't respond.

"It's dinner time. Do you want to take a break?"

I keep reading as she sits on the bed beside me.

"Are you hungry? I could pick something up, bring it back to the room."

Knowing the one-sided conversation will continue, I answer: "Fine."

"I'll be right back."

Once the door clicks shut, I put the letter on my lap. I've read the first sentence three, four, five times. My focus is gone. I refold, place it back in the envelope and then slide it under the rubber bands. How many letters have I read? I count the ones on the bottom—13 letters, 6 cards. I look at the Thanksgiving card again. There's a huge pot of mums on the front–I count seven hues of yellow. Inside she wrote:

When I count my blessings this year, Anna Lee, you are at the top of my list.

I was at the top of Miss June's list. I'd often wondered if Miss June ever thought about me. On lonely nights at my father's house, I wondered if she remembered me at all. And now I know.

I look up at the picture on the wall of a long wooden pier with eight posts on each side, one seagull atop the far-right post. I bet the same painting is in each room. There's probably an identical *everything* in each room: coral bedspread with two decorative pillows, tall desk lamp with coral-striped shade, with two coordinated bedside lamps. Nothing unique.

I close my eyes and see Miss June's face—small, soft, bright. I read the letter again, then move to the next. She's included three pictures and when I flip them over she's made notes in her neat cursive penmanship.

Fun tour through the Red Rocks on the one with her posing next to a pink Jeep. And, *My school* on the photo of a long, one-story building with the red-lettered Sedona Elementary sign in front. I linger on the last picture–Miss June sitting in a blue and white checkered upholstered chair, light from a window on the edge of the frame streaming across her neat, short red hair. She's holding a small stuffed bear with glasses and a tiny white t-shirt that reads: Reading Rocks.

I remember the first time I saw the bear. He was in the window of our local bookstore, posed on top a stack of children's books. Miss June and I were going through our "bear story" phase at the time, reading both fiction and nonfiction stories about imagined and real bears. The bear would be a perfect birthday gift for her.

I was afraid to ask my mother for money to buy a gift for Miss June. Not because we "can't afford it" but because it was for Miss June. It didn't seem right to ask my father, either—it was my gift to her. I raked leaves for our neighbors one Saturday in the fall for tips and had more than enough, so I found another book on bears we hadn't read yet and bought that as well. I turn over the picture.

I miss you more than you'll ever know.

While I read the letters, I keep thinking about how much time I've lost with her, but now I think about how much time Miss June has lost with me. Did she think I read the letters, but didn't want to respond? Or did she think I just tossed them aside?

I'm happy my mother gave me the letters. I'm angry she waited so long. I've been angry with her many, many times before. Somehow I always managed to keep my anger quiet. I instinctively knew my anger could push her over the edge. Back to her old life where wine was a daily focus, not coffee. I'm not sure I can keep my anger quiet this time.

When she returns, I've already placed the letters back inside the box, rearranged the clothes in my suitcase, and placed the box inside. They are mine now. I don't even want her to look at the box.

The food smells good. She opens the paper bag on the desk.

"There's a turkey panini and a caprese sandwich—you pick first," she says, opening the plastic containers.

I take the caprese sandwich and sit by the window again. The light is drawing down outside and the waves are edging further toward the boardwalk.

She's sitting on the side of the first of two double beds in the room, using the nightstand as a table. I hear her take a slow, loud sip from her coffee, followed by a gulp.

"I'm sorry, Anna Lee. I made a mistake."

I look up at her, continuing to eat my sandwich, concentrating on the sweet taste of basil mixed with olive oil.

"I made a mistake, and I'm trying to make it right."

Now I focus on the similarity and differences in the texture of the mozzarella cheese and the firm tomato.

My mother's still talking, and I continue to pay more attention than necessary to my sandwich. I finish and fold my napkin inside the container and toss it in the small trash can.

"It's alright if you don't want to talk to me," she says softly.

I look at her and say the most obvious thing. "Why are you drinking such a small coffee?"

She's holding a tiny cardboard cup with Belvedere stamped in green ink. "I guess you know me," she says. "They were closing but let me place an order. There was only a little coffee left in the pot—just enough to fill their smallest cup."

The sky is getting darker now, but I can still see the waves, the spread of the water covering the smooth sand, then gracefully easing back to the ocean.

"I'm thinking you're not in the mood to go out?" she asks. "Can I stay, or do you want privacy?"

I don't want to rush through the letters. Miss June spent years writing to me, and I want to take my time and read every word.

"I don't want to go out, but you can stay or leave—I don't care," I say, more abruptly than I plan.

My mother sighs—deeply, dramatically.

"I knew you'd be mad. Doesn't it count that I knew you'd be mad, but still decided to give you the letters?"

Suddenly, the light is gone and I can't make out the waves.

"You gave me the letters? You gave me my letters, the ones you stole from me?"

"Oh, Anna Lee. I didn't steal them from you."

"You had something that belonged to me. Isn't that stealing?"

There's an extended silence, but just as my mother opens her mouth, I speak first. "It's selfish. It's selfish to keep something that you knew I would care about. You are a selfish person. Aren't mothers supposed to be unselfish?"

My mother's head darts back, her eyes wide. She opens her mouth again, then closes it. "I'm trying to do the right thing," she says quietly.

I'm not ready to let it go.

"That's what selfish people do. They feel guilty, so they try to make themselves feel better. You only told me now because you knew if Miss June found me, I'm now old enough to go and see her."

Her mouth is open again, and it stays open. She's perfectly still, like she's stopped breathing.

"And if Miss June asks me, I *will* go. I'll live with her. Maybe you'll send me letters and I'll never read them."

My mother makes a small sound—a stifled sob. She looks down and presses the palms of her hands over her eyes. Always so dramatic. She's still holding them there as she speaks.

"I'm going out for a little bit, Anna Lee. Maybe I shouldn't be here right now."

She drops her hands and her makeup is smudged beneath her eyes. She struggles to pull her big purse up to her shoulder and moves to the door, then returns for her key. She turns to me and I know what she's waiting for. *Ask me to stay.* But I don't. Instead, I turn back and focus on the waves I can't see, the moon lighting the heavy gray clouds above.

I hear the door click and pull out my phone and scroll through my contacts. I can't think of a single person to call. A few of my friends have divorced parents, and sometimes they talk about how life changed when their father or mother moved out. But my situation is different. My parents never lived together. Maybe my friends idealized those years their parents were together, but the stories they told were about fun times with both their mothers and fathers: boating weekends, week-long vacations to places like Disney, Yellowstone, the Outer Banks. No one talked about silent fathers and embarrassing mothers. Although since we'd reached high school, I've sensed more of a solidarity with my friends—nearly everyone thought their parents were annoying. Except for Sean.

I didn't date much in high school, and my longest relationship was only six months. It was the second half of my junior year, and Sean was only a sophomore. He wrote poetry and liked to spend time outside—hiking, kayaking, and snowboarding in the winter. I met Sean's family after we'd been dating a couple of months. We had dinner at his house, his older sister and brother, parents, and grandparents all seated around the big oak table—the one Sean and his father built. Laughing, talking over each other, inside jokes, polite questions about my family. I hoped Sean wouldn't invite me again. But he did. Each dinner, barbecue, game night at his house solidified my situation. It wasn't normal. How could I talk to Sean about my mother, my father, Miss June?

My friend Sherry had divorced parents. Her father moved out when she was 10 but rented a house just down the street. They wanted to "co-parent" and put "Sherry's needs first." Even after Sherry's mother remarried, her father came over for birthday parties and other celebrations. I couldn't imagine any circumstance where either of my parents would enter the other's house. Not to celebrate my birthday. Not even my high school graduation.

Nope. I didn't have a single person to call.

Except Miss June.

I wanted to call her after I read the first letter. Then after the second and the third. But I told myself to wait. Wait until I finished reading all the letters. In case there was something in her words that changes my mind.

My phone buzzes. It's my mother, probably thinking she'll apologize from a distance. I'm not going to make this easy for her, so I don't answer.

I start rethinking my decision about calling Miss June later, when my phone buzzes again. This time she leaves a message. A message I don't check.

There's something both exciting and frightening about calling Miss June. Like the start of a roller coaster ride. As I'm going up for the first big drop, there's always the unshakable thought that the cart will derail—fly straight off the metal frame. I thought Miss June rejected me once. Maybe she'll really do it now after I didn't respond to her. It's logical to wait. All the letters so far list her sister's phone number. Maybe she lists her cell phone number on a more recent letter.

My mother calls again, and I know her well enough to realize she'll continue, so I answer. It's another woman's voice.

Chapter 15

"There's been an accident," she says. "The woman…she asked me to call Anna Lee. They're putting her in the ambulance now, and I've got to return her phone."

I feel simultaneously nauseous and dizzy, so I sit on the bed. "Hello?"

"I…where are they taking her? Where are they taking my mother?"

"I'm going to hand the phone to the paramedic; they're getting ready to close the doors."

There's some brief conversation between the woman and a man that I can't make out and two loud metallic clicks.

"Hold on," says a male in an annoyed tone.

I hear a siren and the phone vibrates against something hard. There's more conversation, this time between two men.

"Are you there?" the same male asks. "We're taking her to General. I really can't stay on the phone."

And the call ends.

General I repeat to myself as I grab my purse and room key before heading out to the lobby. I'm breathless by the time I reach the front desk. The clerk is helping a guest, but I walk over to the end of the counter where another employee is sorting papers.

"I need your help," I say. "Is there a hospital called *General*?"

In my mind I sound calm. But judging from the reaction on the woman's face, I realize I'm not in control.

"Yes, of course—do you need directions," she says, pulling over a map. She stops and looks directly at me. "What's wrong?"

"My mother was in an accident—they told me they were taking her to General."

She picks up the phone.

"We need a cab immediately at the Belvedere. To Virginia Beach General. It's an emergency, and would you charge it to our hotel account?"

She nods and hangs up.

"They'll be here in five minutes. You can wait by the door over there until you see the cab pull up. I'd take you myself," she says looking behind her, "but we're short staffed tonight. There's only two of us working." She's taken one of the business cards from the holder on the desk and writes down her name, pushing it toward me. "Here's my name and the hotel number. Call if there's anything I can do for you."

"I...thank you."

I look at my phone four, five, six times before the cab arrives.

"The hospital?" he asks through his open window.

I automatically buckle my seat in the back when I smell it—coffee. The driver has a cup in his console drink holder. As he leaves the curb, I'm looking from side to side, trying to find something to count. And before I can focus on any one thing, we're pulling into the lot.

"Which entrance—front desk or emergency?"

"Emergency."

I'm through the double doors and see the "check in" sign straight ahead. There's a woman with a child there, but they finish just as I arrive.

"My mother, Jacqueline Pierce…brought by ambulance?"

The woman adjusts her glasses and looks at her screen. She pulls a visitor's badge from the stack.

"Straight back through these doors," she says gesturing to her left. "Room 5."

I start back and she calls. "Wait—your visitor's badge." I grab it, but don't bother to clip it to my shirt.

Inside the ER, I'm checking room numbers—15, 14, 13. I realize I should have turned in the opposite direction when I entered, but I continue to circle around the center hub, where doctors and nurses are up and down, looking at charts and computer screens, crossing from the staff section to the patient rooms. An invisible line between healthy and not healthy.

I'm almost there—7, 6. And then there's 5. The bed is empty. I just stand there, staring at the bed. There's no sign of my mother in this room. No purse, no clothes. Maybe she gave me the wrong room number. Maybe they admitted her to the hospital and she's on another floor. Maybe…

"Can I help you?"

There's a young nurse behind me, wearing scrubs with a high-heeled shoe print, her blonde hair pulled back from her face.

"My mother—Jacqueline Pierce. They told me…"

She puts her hand on my shoulder.

"Yes, come in here and have a seat," she says guiding me into the room. "They'll have her back shortly. She's getting some scans."

"Do you want the TV on," she asks at the door.

"No—thank you."

I'm sitting in the chair, but the room is tilting, back and forth. I concentrate on breathing as I scan the room for color. I count three shades of white. Maybe not actual shades, more like variations probably based on when the walls were painted, or bleached clean. They must bleach everything; it's a hospital. Finally, I discover a medium gray and a dark gray on the equipment, and I start to settle a little. What happened in the last few hours? My silence. My anger. My words. *You are a selfish person.*

There's a noisy piece of equipment in one of the nearby rooms, and I start to count the beeps and quickly detect a pattern. After every five beeps, there's a slightly longer pause. I'm wondering if the equipment is defective and how that could affect the patient.

"Oh, Anna Lee!"

The wheelchair isn't fully in the door and I'm up and holding her hand—softly, tentatively.

"Are you alright?"

"Let's get her in bed," says the young woman who is pushing her into the room. "You'll have to let go of her hand for a minute."

The woman locks the wheelchair and navigates her onto the thin mattress.

"Are you comfortable? I can raise the—"

"No—perfect," my mother says. "Just perfect."

We're alone and I sit on the side of the bed, holding her hand again.

"I'm sorry," she says, looking directly at me.

"Why are you sorry? I'm the one who should be sorry. I didn't mean—"

"This certainly isn't the way I wanted to spend our time together," she says.

We sit quietly for a moment. I can hear the beeps again and I'm counting—1, 2, 3, 4, 5, slight pause...

"I bet they don't even have good coffee here," she laughs.

"Maybe they have the best coffee—the best you've had so far," I say. "Wouldn't that be ironic? You're looking for the best cup of coffee and you find it here?"

"Doubtful. Although the ER is busy around the clock. Something must keep those doctors and nurses awake for the night shift."

"What did the doctor say?"

"Oh, Anna Lee. I'm fine. They're just making sure so I won't sue them later."

"I don't think it works that way."

I realize I don't know anything about the accident. In the cab, I had thoughts of her speeding down the street, thinking about what I said.

"What happened?"

"Another driver wasn't paying attention—on his cell phone. You know that's why I always tell you not to look at your cell phone while you're driving. No one thinks they'll be distrac–"

"Where did he hit you—I mean the car?"

"He pulled out from one of the side streets, hit the other door pretty hard. It jolted me and my head hit the window. Someone stopped and when they saw me rubbing my head, they called an ambulance."

"I'm thankful it wasn't worse," I say quietly.

She lifts her face, and there's a brightness.

"Thank God you weren't sitting in that passenger's seat," she says. "You don't know how grateful I am that you didn't go with me."

Chapter 16

It's 1 a.m. and we're finally back at the hotel. I'm too tired to feel anything, but as I pass between exhaustion and rest, I replay one of the day's scenes. Not the scene when my mother told me about the letters. Not the scene of my anger that followed. The scene I remember is at the hospital—the doctor's serious face when she returned.

"Hello, young lady. Would you mind stepping out into the lobby to wait for your mother? We'll have someone bring her out when we're finished."

The doctor didn't look at me or my mother; she was staring at her tablet, which I assumed carried all of my mother's information.

"It's okay, I'll be out shortly," my mother said. "Maybe you can find a number for the cab company. We'll call when I'm finished."

I walked slowly, but the constant churn of the equipment and other voices around me covered any conversation in the room.

Now in bed, just as I think I'll never fall asleep with all the racing thoughts, I feel myself drifting off. And I'm dreaming of the ocean. I'm floating in the heat of day, when the sun sets in a flash and the moon rises. The waves are like shadowed clouds around me, beneath me. And suddenly they are over me. Churning, churning.

I stretch my arms to both sides but there's only water. I keep reaching for someone, something. I'm on my own. I pull the water with my hands and swim, hopeful that each carefully executed stroke will lead me back to the surface. Somehow the water is more powerful than even my best strokes, and I'm swirling beneath a murky surface when I see a needle-thin ray of moonlight coming from a different direction. Should I follow my instincts and continue, or should I move toward the unknown—that tiny light in the distance?

There's a familiar, comforting scent, and I open my eyes to daylight. My mother has already picked up coffee from downstairs, and is sipping loudly, looking out the window. I make the slightest of shifts in my bed.

"You're up! Are you hungry?"

I choke back a laugh. I'm not hungry. But she's probably ready for a second cup of coffee.

"I'll get ready."

"No hurry. I just thought you'd be ready for something to eat. It's almost 10."

I can't imagine the self-will it took for my mother to restrain herself from waking me. She used to be quiet in the mornings. But more recently, she'd rotate through a selection of morning inspirations, all with a goal to get me out of bed.

Don't sleep your life away, sleepy head!

The sunshine is waiting for you!

Rise and shine!

Make this your best day yet!

Carpe Diem, Anna Lee! And just to drive it home, she'd add: *Seize the Day!*

Today, my mother let me sleep in. She didn't recite her mantras or break into song. Maybe it would be a beautiful day after all.

I'm in the bathroom brushing my teeth when I realize I forgot to ask how she's feeling. I shake my head. Which one of us is selfish? I try to brush my hair quickly, but it's knotted, like I spent the night tossing in my sleep.

"How are you feeling?" I ask, emerging from the bathroom dressed and ready.

"Oh, I'm fine, Ann Lee," she says looking at me closely. "I have some undereye cream if you'd like to use it."

I laugh. "I guess you really are fine!"

Downstairs, it's the lull between the breakfast and lunch crowd at the coffee shop, so we find a seat by the window with a view of the boardwalk. It's a weekday in fall, so the beachgoing crowds are mostly gone. A family rides by on a carriage bicycle, the parents in the front peddling their young children in the back seat. A dark-skinned man with dreadlocks and a t-shirt with a drawing of a faded, lemon-yellow sun walks by slowly, smiling as the family passes him. There are two girls around my age, one blonde and overly tanned, and the other black haired with naturally tan skin, both dressed in a brown uniform, walking quickly like they are late for their shift at some restaurant.

"Are you still serving *breakfast*?" my mother asks.

The young waitress, whose tangled hair and smeared mascara make her look like she's been up all night, points to a banner in large letters on the menu: *Breakfast served all day.*

"Not sure how I missed that!" my mother laughs. "Well, I'll have a large coffee and a veggie omelet, with breakfast potatoes, please. Anna Lee?"

"I'll have a green tea and a veggie omelet as well, but with egg whites."

"Will get those right up for you," she says, without writing anything down and taking our menus.

A gray-haired couple walks by, holding hands. Their shirts are an identical shade of cornflower blue with slightly different inscriptions.

Her: *Best Grammy Ever*

His: *Best Poppy Ever*

My mother notices them too.

She clears her throat. "Have you ever thought about… would you like to know more about your grandparents? I've never talked about either one of them much."

She never talked about them at all.

"Yes—of course. I've always wondered about them; what they were like."

Maybe she bumped her head harder in the accident than she's admitting.

She sighs loudly. "If it's all the same, we'll talk about them tomorrow. Today, we need to look into car repairs."

I nod. What's another day?

"They towed my car to a local body shop. After we finish our breakfast, do you want to stay here while I grab a cab there? I'll find out how long the repairs are going to take."

I remember the unread letters upstairs.

"Yeah, I'll just hang around here."

"Coffee and green tea," the waitress says, putting the cups in the wrong places.

We just smile. After the woman walks away, my mother switches the cups.

"She thinks I drink green tea!" my mother says. "Do I look like someone who drinks green tea?"

I laugh. "What's that supposed to mean?"

"You Anna Lee—you are clearly the green tea drinker at this table. Can you imagine me switching to green tea? My friends would think I'd lost my mind."

She was right. Everyone who knew anything about my mother knew her favorite beverage. Although, it wasn't always her favorite beverage. That's another secret from her past that she's keeping from me. Except I already know.

I'm alone with the letters again. The full sun warms my face by the window as I settle in the chair and slide out the next letter from the stack. I run my finger across the name and address and turn it over, smiling as I see another tiny ladybug on the flap. A memory flashes—black patent leather shoes with little ladybugs lined up on the straps. Did Miss June buy those for me? And a little black purse with a circle of ladybugs. I remember trying to keep it on my shoulder, the black cord sliding down my arm.

The flap is sealed firmly, so I tear the side of the envelope and feel a sharp paper cut. It's starting to bleed so I grab a tissue out of the box on the desk and wrap it around a couple of times. I wish I had a pair of scissors. Inside, there's another picture, but Miss June's not in it. I recognize the setting instantly and she confirms on the back: *Day trip to Grand Canyon.* I count slowly. There are at least eight different shades of brown. And at least four reds and three yellows—more golden than yellow.

I remember a similar picture on Miss June's refrigerator, held in place by a "Reading is Fundamental" magnet that the library gave out one summer. Her sister, May was wearing a canvas hat with a drawstring pulled under her chin, posed in front of the same view. She had been leaning back on the railing, one that must have kept countless visitors from falling in the deep crevasse. How long would it take to hit the ground?

Five seconds? Ten seconds? Longer? Or was there a ridge just below, a kind of "Plan B" in case the railing gave way?

When Miss June received the photo in the mail, she told me that May rode a mule to the bottom. I was horrified, but apparently, they had the best safety record—much better than hikers who slid off the narrow trail. Miss June said we might take a mule ride there when I was older. I wasn't convinced.

I unfold the letter and read:

Anna Lee,

As you'll see in the photo, I finally discovered a place the two of us talked about visiting. As I expected, the size is impossible to capture in a photo—or even a whole series of photos! I wish you were here to describe the colors you see in the rock and dirt. Looking at this photo I've enclosed, I realize the camera is so limited. It's impossible to distinguish between the subtle shades. I can distinguish some, but it takes someone with your eyes, your gift to fully translate.

I didn't take the mule ride. I'm saving that for when you come to visit.

Love, Miss June

In previous letters, Miss June wrote that she'd like me to visit. In this one, she said "when."

I take a deep breath, and follow my now-established process—carefully folding the letter, placing it back in the envelope, and moving it to the bottom of the stack. The letters were like the box of perfectly presented Belgian chocolates Miss June and my father gave me after they returned from a getaway to Chicago. They were so delicious, I wanted to eat the entire box at once. Instead, I decided to eat one a day to let the flavor last longer.

My mother's phone is buzzing. She's left it behind again. I'm surprised there's still battery life because she forgets to charge it as well. I hear the sound for voice mail, and when I check the phone, two messages have been left from the same number with our home area code. I press the icon for the messages and listen.

I play each message twice. The second almost identical to the first. The messages don't make sense. Unless my mother lied. I want to delete the messages, pretend they were never recorded. Pretend she's not keeping yet one more secret.

Chapter 17

When my mother opens the door, she's balancing two cups of coffee in a cardboard caddy in her right hand, her big red purse over her left wrist.

"No car yet," she says. "But the good news is, we'll have it by the time they close, or early tomorrow morning at the latest."

She sets the cardboard tray on the desk.

"I found the cutest little spot for coffee, just a short walk from the repair shop," she said. "Thought you might be ready for an iced coffee!"

"Why did you lie?" I ask so quietly I can barely hear myself.

"What?"

I raise my voice. "Why did you lie?"

My mother inhales, and frowns.

"Oh, Anna Lee. I'm not sure what else I can say about those letters. I've said I was sorry. I've given you the letters. I'm not sure what else you expect."

"I'm not talking about the letters."

"Then what is it? Not telling you about your grandparents?"

"It's not about any of that. It's not about anything that happened before. It's about what's happening now."

My mother looks away from me and sits down on the bed.

There's a few beats of quiet before I continue.

"The accident. Why don't you tell me what really happened?"

"I don't know what you mean," she says, her voice low.

"Your insurance company called."

My mother's giant purse is on her lap, and she immediately starts feeling around with one hand.

"You left your phone here," I say.

"And you answered it? It's my phone. You expect privacy, and I expect it too. Why did you think it was alright–"

"It's not about me right now. It's about you. The insurance company said it was a single car collision. What did you hit? A tree?"

My mother is looking down again.

"It was a telephone pole."

"On the sidewalk?"

"Yes. It happened so quickly. Thankfully, the curb slowed me down, so I was barely moving when I hit the pole."

My mind races ahead, and I ask, "Were you drinking?"

My mother's face drops, her eyes dark and narrow. Her mouth freezing momentarily.

"No," she says quietly. "I wasn't drinking, Anna Lee."

She puts her purse on the bed, and moves over to the other bed, the one that's next to where I'm sitting at the window. She's still looking down when she starts talking.

"Okay, I guess it's time. One more thing to be sorry about. I guess it was unrealistic, naive of me to think you didn't remember. That you were too young. I haven't had a drink for a long time."

Maybe it's my need to trust her, but I believe she's telling me the truth.

"Do you still think about it? Is it hard?"

She nods. "Everyday."

I expect her to make a joke about coffee being her replacement addiction, but she doesn't. So I make the joke myself.

"I guess coffee helps?"

She smiles. "Coffee helps. But you help more. You were the reason I stopped and you are the reason that I don't drink— each day. You are the reason."

I get up and pull her coffee from the tray.

"Here. Have a sip," I say.

She takes a long drink.

"Thanks, Anna Lee."

"About that car accident," I start.

"I guess we're still on that," she says, smiling slightly. "A homeless woman darted out in the street. As soon as I saw her, I hit the brake and turned my wheel toward the sidewalk. I remember hitting the curb...I'm starting to remember hitting the pole."

Inside the room there's a dull hum. A creak on the bed as my mother adjusts herself. The click of the elevator doors closing in the hall. I think I hear the waves churning on the beach, but the thick window glass that separates the beige room from the grays and blues and silvers of the surf also separates the sounds.

On our first day, I tried to slide the window open, but it wouldn't budge. Like most hotels, the windows were permanently closed. I'd been told they were sealed to prevent people from suicide. People couldn't leap out the window. They couldn't float away with the spray of saltwater on their faces, listening to the glorious crash of waves on the shore. But they could float away by carving a deep ridge in their wrists, swallowing poison, or taking a handful of prescription pills, all inside these beige walls with the sound of a dull hum surrounding them as they left everything behind.

My mother takes my hand, but I'm still confused about the accident.

"Why didn't you just tell me what happened—why did you lie about the accident?"

The bed creaks again and my mother releases my hand. I count 16 seconds of silence before she answers.

"You were so angry at me. I didn't want you to be angrier than you already were. I just knew you'd think I was careless."

I nod, but it still doesn't seem right. Why would I be mad that my mother risked her life to save someone who was in the street? Sometimes her logic doesn't make sense. I'm unrealistic to think she might change. Better to let this one go. There was enough mystery with Miss June's letters and the story of my grandparents. I hoped the tiny pressure in the back of my brain, that signaled me something wasn't right, would eventually go away.

Chapter 18

I'm counting again. We've just crossed over the invisible border between Virginia and North Carolina, according to the *Welcome* sign. So far, I've counted 11 North Carolina license plates, but I'm expecting that number to increase quickly when my mother interrupts my focus.

"Here we go, Anna Lee—another state on our Coffee by Car!"

I'm reminded of my journal. And even though she is right next to me in the driver's seat, I add more evidence that confirms my mother is crazy:

#4 Hits a telephone pole and lies about it.

#5 Hides my personal letters from Miss June.

I consider writing *steals my father from her best friend* but decide to be generous. After all, Miss June and my father eventually married, even if it wasn't a perfect match.

Earlier today, we packed, checked out of the hotel, and took an Uber to the repair shop. Not much change. The old chipped paint and rust spots were still there. Good thing Jeeps are nearly indestructible.

She's turning down the music.

"Well, this time I don't have a coffee spot in mind, so we're going without a plan!"

I raise my eyebrows and open my mouth, but close it to resist responding.

"Would you check your phone and find us another beach town?"

I do a search on North Carolina beaches and click on a map. Wrightsville Beach looks like a short drive away, and when I search for coffee shops, there's a place on the beach that looks promising. A little shack of a restaurant: Fins Place. It's more breakfast and lunch, but they do mention *free coffee while you wait on the wraparound porch.*

There's still some time before we get there. The box of letters is tucked into my suitcase now, so I decide to unwrap a different kind of envelope. The secret she's been keeping about my grandparents.

"Is this a good time to tell me about your mom and dad?"

There's a pause so long that I think she's gone situationally deaf—just long enough to ignore my question.

Then her usual, dramatic sigh. And a second one. As though she's sending me a signal: Caution—emotionally draining information ahead!

"I suppose so, Anna Lee. Let's see where to start..."

I adjust the lever on the side of the seat to slight recline and close my eyes for a second to prepare. No more counting license plates.

"I was born in a small town just outside Asheville, North Carolina. My mother was an accountant for one of the tobacco companies, but she quit just before I was born. My father was a professor at the junior college near our house. When I was little, I remember him walking home between classes to have lunch with us."

"You were an only child—right?"

I'd asked my mother once if she had a brother or sister and she shook her head, but there was something in her reaction that made me wonder.

"Well. I try not to think about this, but my mother was pregnant with twins," she says, her voice so deep it's not familiar.

I don't know why I continue to be surprised. My mother had siblings. And kept them a secret.

"After you were born? Or before?"

"No—neither," she said. "My twin brother was pronounced dead when he was born."

"Oh, that's sad–your poor parents!"

"It was sad for me," my mother said quickly. "Imagine how different my life would have been. Sometimes when I close my eyes I can see him. I told your father that once and he thought I was crazy. I told June too."

"Did she think you were crazy?"

"June? No, she didn't think I was crazy. She said she believed me."

"How long did your brother live—a few minutes, an hour?"

"He actually died before I was born. While we were still in our mother's womb. The doctor knew something was wrong and sent my mother to a specialist in Asheville. He was already dead at least a month before I was born, but it was too dangerous to do anything but wait for the delivery."

I'm still processing. My mother in the womb with her dead brother. Maybe that made her crazy from the very start.

"Did your parents name him—your brother?"

She smiles. "Henry. Henry James."

I repeat the name a couple of times.

"I like that. It's a solid name. At least your parents didn't give you matching names."

I knew two sets of twins from school: Molly and Melody; Suzette and Bridgette. Jacqueline and Henry–no first letter matches or rhymes.

"Did your parents have any other children?"

"No—just me and Henry. My parents didn't really talk about him, at least when I was around. It's so odd, even thinking about it now. One night when my mother said prayers with me, she said, 'We should pray for Henry.'"

"Did you ask her who Henry was?"

"No—I just looked up and asked—Henry my brother?"

"Wow—that must have shocked her!"

"That's the odd part, Anna Lee. She didn't seem surprised at all. Like she expected me to know Henry. After that night, she mentioned him sometimes. But not in a sad way. Once we were at the zoo, and she asked me which animal was my favorite. Then she asked me which animal would be Henry's favorite."

"Did your father do that?" I ask. "Talk about Henry?"

"No Anna Lee. Not even once."

She looks up for a moment. Hesitates. And I wonder if something's just coming to her for the first time.

"He never mentioned him by name, but my father remembered him. All the time."

She put her sunglasses on her lap and wiped her eyes with the back of her hand.

"Recently, I've thought more about my father. I think his silence changed him. My mother didn't mention Henry often, but when she did, she seemed brighter. My father just grew darker—more isolated with each year. It took me a long time to put all that together," she says, putting her sunglasses back on.

We drive quietly for a while, then my mother starts the story again, picking up at the same place, like she's bookmarked the page.

"There was a heaviness about my father, like energy was slowly draining from his body. He stopped coming home for lunch and rarely spent time with me. No after dinner walk around the neighborhood. No evening bedtime story. No weekly trip to the library.

"One night as my mother sat on the edge of my bed, saying prayers with me, I heard cupboards opening and shutting and my father's raised, almost desperate voice: 'Where did you put it?' My mother kissed me and shut the door behind her, but I could still hear her quiet voice: 'It's right here—I just moved some things…' Then a clink of glass that I came to expect every night."

"Your father was an alcoholic."

She nods. "The bottle became a replacement for my brother. One evening after dinner, I was probably ten or eleven, I asked him if we could take a walk. One of my school friends had a new puppy. My father sometimes mentioned Sadie, the collie he had as a child, and I thought if my father saw the puppy, the sadness would lift. Unrealistic, I know."

My mother takes her hand off the wheel for a moment, then puts it back quickly. I don't think she wants me to see that her hand is shaking.

"I waited for an answer and even though he didn't say anything, he gave me one. My father walked over to the cupboard, pulled out the bottle and a glass and poured himself a drink. I can still see the amber liquid splashing into his short, crystal glass."

"What did your mother do?"

"First, she put the bottle back in the cupboard. She always put it back, even though my father always left it on the counter. Then, she took me on that walk to see the puppy. She walked faster than usual, and I wondered if we were going to keep walking. Walking away from the house, away from my father."

"Did that happen—did she ever leave him?"

"No Anna Lee, life there never changed," she answers. "That night in bed, when I heard the cupboard door open and shut and the clink of the glass, my mind opened to a single thought. One that took me a long time to form, and one that would never go away: I wasn't enough for my father."

I want to speak, to say something that will contradict her, but the words get caught in my throat and I'm afraid I'll cry. I count road signs instead. The mile markers, exit signs, advertising billboards, the large green overhead signs announcing the number of miles to upcoming towns—I count them all. I'm up to 22 when she continues.

"He gets worse. He gets darker and angrier. Less predictable. He never hits me, but his words feel like he's hitting me. Tells me I can't do anything right. Over, and over again. Sometimes he just asks a question, looking right through me, 'Why YOU?'"

"What does that mean?"

"It means he wishes I was the twin who died."

The air is hot in the car, and I lower my window and wipe my hands on the front of my shorts.

"And your mother?"

"He doesn't yell at me when my mother is there, and I never tell her. As time goes by, she grows sadder and quieter. And finally, I start high school. I never invite anyone to my house. And when I ask if I can stay overnight with a friend, my mother always says yes. She seems relieved," she shifts in the seat and adjusts the sun visor.

"By my senior year, my father isn't Department Head anymore, teaching fewer classes. My mother tells people he's transitioning to retirement. She volunteers at the library, spends even more time there when my father is home. But she starts timing her returns to make sure I'm not alone with my father. Like she knows how he treats me when she's away."

It's hard for me to imagine my mother living that way. She's so strong. It's hard to imagine that she didn't run away.

"I was seeing Jimmy, a sweet guy who lived just a few streets away. I introduced him to my father the first time we went out, but made sure it was early in the day—a Saturday morning. Most times when he picked me up, I was at the door waiting for him. Sometimes I even waited outside."

My mother takes a deep breath and exhales with a long puff.

"It's late in the school year and I'm at the movies with Jimmy. My mother wasn't feeling well all day and was in bed when I left the house. She got worse. She had a sharp pain in her side that grew to agony. My father somehow managed to get her in the car for the short drive to the hospital. He didn't call an ambulance."

She says those last words like she's still trying to figure out why he decided to drive, rather than make the call.

"Had he been drinking?" I ask slowly.

"He had, Anna Lee. Like every day for as long as I can remember. Of course he'd been drinking."

I almost ask my mother to stop. Maybe I don't want her to go through the pain of saying it. Or maybe I just don't want to hear it. She doesn't need to tell me that her father had an accident. That her mother was tragically injured.

"He'd been drinking, and he didn't call an ambulance. So he got behind the wheel with the person in my life who loved me the most. The person who I loved the most. And he ran the stop sign. And the car that had the right-of-way at that intersection crashed at full speed into the passenger side. Full speed into my mother."

Chapter 19

I wish I hadn't asked her about my grandparents. My mother is crying and all I can do is awkwardly cross my arms, even though I know they should be wrapped around her. She wipes her eyes, takes a deep breath and continues.

"She was gone and there was nothing I could do to change that, no matter how many times I thought about that day. When I play that scene in my mind, which I've done countless times over the years, I imagine my mother in pain, doubled over, looking down. I tell myself she didn't see the car coming. She didn't feel the impact. She was killed instantly. The other driver, an elderly woman on her way to pick up her grand-daughter from work at our local drug store, was killed as well. My father had no serious injuries. Two people died, but he had no serious injuries," she says with an awkward, short laugh. "Where's the fairness in that?"

"What happened to your father? Was he arrested?"

"No, Anna Lee. Things were different then. Small town, protect the people you know. I doubt anyone even thought to charge him. The Police Chief and likely many of the officers were students of my father at one time. An ambulance responded to the scene and took him to the hospital—just to check him out. When I heard the story, I realized it was probably the same ambulance that would have transported my mother to the hospital. And she'd still be alive."

The next road sign shows we're getting closer to the exit for Wrightsville Beach. And I still have questions.

"You blamed him?"

My mother looks at me quickly, frowning, her face red. She takes a long deep breath and then a second.

"At first I blamed myself as much as I blamed him. If I'd only stayed home that day. I usually didn't talk about my father, but I opened up to Jimmy's mother. She helped me realize I wasn't the one to blame. So yes, I blamed him, Anna Lee. For a long time. It was only in the past few years that I was able to forgive him."

"What changed?"

My mother sighs. "I changed, or at least I like to think so. I'm still working my way through the 12 steps in my recovery, but taking a personal inventory helped. The forgiveness was about freeing myself, but it was also an acceptance that my father was a broken man. And that we're all broken people. Broken in different ways. We make the best decisions we can at the time. Even though, looking back, they may have been the worst decisions. And not just the worse decisions for ourselves, but for the people we love the most."

She glances at me. Is she still talking about her father?

"Have you tried to call him?"

"It's too late. I'd finally gotten to the point where I was ready to think about forgiveness. Not sure I could do it, but ready to think about it. I'd even contacted Belinda, the daughter of his cousin who still lives near Asheville. She gave me the address and phone number at the senior housing where he'd lived for many years. And I planned to call. Every night I'd tell myself I'd make the call the next day. But I never did."

"It's not too late," I say gently. "We could go there now."

"I thought about that. First, I decided to drive down myself and see him. Then another month went by. Then I thought I'd drive down with you, so you could meet him. But I wasn't ready to tell you the story yet. More months went by. And then Belinda called. I waited too long."

I motion with my hand toward the exit; she turns and I navigate her toward Fins Place. When we arrive, there are a few people sipping from white mugs on the front porch.

"I think I need that cup of coffee," my mother says as she parks.

When we get out of the car, she doesn't head directly to the familiar warmth and aroma like I expect. She wraps her arms around me, tentatively at first, then firmly. And she doesn't let go. I feel myself tensing up at first, but then my whole body relaxes into hers.

"I love you, Anna Lee."

"I know. I love you too."

She pulls me even closer before letting go. And then, she's quickly striding up the steps toward the coffee.

My mother's in the door before I make it up the stairs. I find a seat on the porch along the benches around the edge. The tide is coming in and the waves wash the small, makeshift beach, the sun reflecting sparkles on the tiny specks of stone in the sand.

There's no one my age on the porch. To my right is a group of women a bit older than my mother, wearing bright cover-ups in various tones of aqua, coral, and yellow. One of them is standing, telling a story. When she gets to the punchline, she nearly shouts it: *He said—but I've never even met you!* And the women laugh and laugh. One of them laughs so hard she upsets the coffee mug at her feet, which causes even more laughter.

My mother arrives with two of the plain white mugs and a cardboard cup.

"I'm sorry, Anna Lee. No green tea. No iced coffee. I only added cream to yours. But I've got a couple sugar packets if you need to sweeten. And, I did manage a cup of ice. You can make your own."

"Thank you," I say taking both the mug and the ice, which she's balancing in one hand.

I add a few cubes and sip.

"It fine," I say, waving away the white sugar packets she's holding up.

"We have a short wait," she says. "About twenty minutes. The place is packed, so I guess that's a good sign! Are you hungry?"

I nod.

It feels good to transition to an easier topic for a few minutes, even though I want to know more about my grandparents. I take out my phone and pull up the menu. "Looks like mostly seafood, but a good variety."

"Well, what else would we eat at the beach," she says laughing. "I could never understand why your father didn't like seafood. I mean really—I understand some people don't like fish, but no crab or shrimp?"

"It's true," I say, rolling my eyes. "I once asked him if he was allergic. I don't think I know anyone who doesn't eat seafood."

Even Hannah ate seafood. She was one of my friends from school, although we weren't as close as we used to be. But she was definitely my oldest friend—I met her on my first day of kindergarten. At some point in our sophomore year of high school, she proclaimed herself a vegetarian, but continued to eat seafood. Several of us tried to convince Hannah that she wasn't really a vegetarian if she ate seafood, but she wouldn't listen.

"I don't eat animals," she'd say.

Apparently, she didn't categorize fish, crab, shrimp, oysters, clams, or even lobsters as animals. And nothing we could say would change her mind. Our friend Tanni proclaimed her a pollotarian. The rest of us didn't know what that meant, so we looked it up later, learning that pollotarians don't eat red meat and do eat seafood. But they also eat chicken. When we looked further, we decided the term pescatarian was a solid fit—someone who didn't eat red meat or chicken, but did eat seafood. Hannah still wouldn't agree.

"Nope. I'm a vegetarian," she'd say, no matter what the facts showed.

My father was the opposite of Hannah. He ate lots of red meat and chicken and no seafood. I wonder if there was a term for people like that. He also ate very few vegetables, but had a couple exceptions—he loved potatoes and green beans. And apple sauce, although that didn't really count as a vegetable even though the carry-out menus always showed it with the salad and steamed broccoli.

"Jack-CAW-line?" the lady with long, straight brown hair and a thick swatch of gray roots calls from the entrance.

Inside, the restaurant is about what I expect. Plastic crabs and fish painted unnatural colors and mounted on walls. Netting strung from one corner to the middle of the wall, captured starfish inside. I can't tell if they're real or not, but judging from the rest of the plastic, I'm guessing they were purchased at some tourist shop. We're seated at a sturdy wood table for two, the chairs so heavy, they're hard to move close to the table.

"Would y'all like to hear our specials?"

She runs through the list, without prices, then points out the sections of the menu. Our waitress, Nell is an elderly, round woman with curly gray hair. She's staring curiously at my mother's braids.

"Did y'all just get back from the Bahamas?" she asks.

My mother's lips part, then close. She purses them together, a sign that she's confused. Then she breaks into laughter and brushes back her braids.

"Oh, these?" she asks smiling as the woman nods. "I like to tell people I have them because I'm creative, but maybe I'm just lazy!"

Then they both laugh.

I already know I want seafood, but I'm losing focus as I read all the options—24 seafood options in all including the appetizers, sandwiches, entrees, and even a salmon salad. I'm still not sure if I want the lightly breaded Cod sandwich, but I want to order something quickly so my mother will finish telling me about my grandparents. She's still flipping pages back and forth. Nell has already refilled the coffee mug, so there's no sense of urgency—my mother has what she needs. It's clear she's stalling and part of me doesn't want to rush her. But I have an overwhelming feeling that this might be the only chance I'll have to uncover yet another of her secrets.

Chapter 20

She taps the tip of her index finger, the red polish now starting to chip, on one selection and then another. She purses her lips again.

"What's the difference between this shrimp plate and the other?"

I turn to the page.

"One is fried, the other steamed."

"Or do I feel like fish?" she asks.

"Well, I feel like eating. Aren't you ready to order yet?" I ask, slightly under my breath, but loud enough to be heard.

"OK, Anna Lee," she laughs. "I forgot it's been awhile since we've eaten." She looks at Nell. "Sorry, I'll just need another minute," then back at me apologetically.

I force myself to stay quiet while she looks at the menu, but when she closes it, I'm ready with a question.

"What happened after the accident? Did your father change?"

My mother sighs and shakes her head.

"Not in any meaningful way. He was already withdrawn, and that didn't improve. I suppose the timing was fortunate for me. The next fall I started college."

She takes a long sip from her coffee, then leans back in the dark wood chair.

"Although my original plans shifted. I planned to attend the college where my father taught. Tuition was free for children of faculty. Instead, I took out a student loan that took me years to pay off. That's how I ended up in New Jersey. When my father realized I was going to school out of state, he suggested a small private college. I chose a large public college instead. He thought I should major in education. I chose journalism."

"Did he visit you while you were in college?"

"He didn't visit. I really believed he would. Believed he could hold it together for one weekend. I spent Parents' Weekend my freshman year crying in my room. I sent him the invitation and even called a week in advance to remind him."

"Did you go home on your breaks?"

"I went home my first Christmas. On my train ride back home, I imagined the bleakest holiday possible. My prediction turned out to be accurate. There was a tree in the living room—I found out later that Belinda and her mother, bless them, set it up. The box of ornaments was sitting to the side. They must have thought my father and I would want to decorate the tree together. Maybe the tree was too much of a reminder of what we'd lost. To tell you the truth, I opened the ornament box, took out a couple of the ornaments then replaced them and shut the lid. My mother was everything good about Christmas. She had a story about each one of the ornaments—the ones I made for her in school, the ones we collected on trips. It was all just too much, especially the first year after her death."

"What about the next year?"

"I went home that summer, but didn't spend much time at the house. I worked as a nanny for a couple that traveled a lot, so I spent most of my time at their house. By the next Christmas, I had a job on campus. I never went home again."

"Your graduation? Did he come?"

"Said he would, Anna Lee. Said he had a hotel room reserved and had mapped out the route. I suppose that was true. When the time came, I guess he just couldn't do it."

"That must have been hard. Wasn't it...hard not to have anyone there for graduation?"

"I had people there. My roommate's parents had become like family to me. Latrice...did you know she was my college roommate?"

I nodded. I think Latrice was the reason my mother started wearing braids. They sometimes referred to themselves as sisters. Only the braids didn't look garish in Latrice's thick black hair.

"Truth be told, I was relieved he didn't come. Relieved I didn't have to introduce my father to my friends, my professors, Latrice's family. Relieved they wouldn't see him stagger, smell the alcohol, hear him slur his words."

She empties her cup with a final, long drink and immediately begins looking for the waitress, sliding the mug to the end of the table.

"I'm sorry I couldn't tell you something wonderful, inspiring about your grandfather. But your grandmother—she was all good things. Your grandmother was special. Elizabeth Anna. Her maiden name was Lee–you were named after her. She really was one of those people who everyone loved. Although I've always wondered if my father was the exception."

She sighs.

"I guess I shouldn't make that assumption. He didn't treat anyone well. Maybe he wasn't capable. Or maybe it was only because of the alcohol. I've thought a lot about my parents over the last year. Maybe with couples, there's only so much goodness between them—and my mother got it all."

That couldn't possibly be true based on my parents.

"My mother constantly looked for ways to make peoples' lives better. She tutored children and college students for free, and even tutored our neighbor, Miss Amy. She was a 'War Bride' from Germany who spoke English fairly well, but couldn't read it. My mother worked with her for years, and I saw how much my mother changed Miss Amy's life. She asked friends for their recipes, subscribed to the daily newspaper, and even read books with her children. That's just one person. I'd spend the rest of the trip telling you the difference she made in so many lives. Part of mourning my mother was mourning all the good she would have done the rest of her life."

Nell fills my mother's mug. She glances at me, and I shake my head.

"Are you ladies ready to order?" she asks.

We both order shrimp plates—steamed (me), fried (her).

My mother's taking another long sip, even though steam is rising. She puts her mug down and leans back in her chair.

"As hard as it was to accept that she wouldn't be there for all those other people, it was even harder for me to accept she wouldn't be there for me anymore. When I was deciding on my college classes, when a relationship fell apart, when I was applying for a job, when I had you..."

She looks down for a moment and sniffles, then uses her paper napkin to wipe her eyes.

"It's a long list, Anna Lee. What's the hardest for me is knowing your life would have been so much better if she were still here. Because *I* would have been so much better."

I wish I still had the menu, so I'd have something to look at. Instead, I stare at the people who sit behind my mother—two men in polo shirts who look like they've come from a golf course. There are two bottles of beer on their table, and two glasses—but only one is using his glass.

"A heavier conversation than you were expecting?" my mother asks.

"Uh-huh. Definitely."

"We can take a break."

"Were there ever happier times in your childhood?" I ask. "Any good times with both your mom and dad?"

My mother's tight lips relax.

"There were a few," she said. "Probably more than a few. Especially when he wasn't drinking. There were times when he held it together—days, weeks."

She looks to the side, her face slightly scrunched.

"We took a trip once to New York City. I was only about 4 at the time, so I'm not sure how much I actually remember. My mother talked about the trip over the years, and would pull out one of our photo albums to remind me. I loved that silky pink coat I wore. Made me feel so grown up, so cosmopolitan," she laughs. "My mother took a picture of me at every major attraction. I'm posed in front of the Statue of Liberty, a garden in Central Park, the Empire State Building, and even one of the subway entrances."

"I'd love to see those pictures—do you still have them?"

"I do. I took a couple of albums with me when I left for college."

"Both your parents went?" I ask.

"They did. Must have been before he started drinking —or at least started drinking heavily. There's a sweet picture of my father, me lifted on his side shoulder as he holds me by the waist. I'm holding my hand up waving. And there are other pictures in the albums. One fall we went camping in the Blue Ridge Mountains. The trees, the overlooks—I don't think I've ever seen any place so beautiful my whole life. Or at least, that's how I remember it."

"Tent camping? You went tent camping?" I ask, smiling.

"I did, just that once. It was the three of us—our sleeping bags and small canvas tent borrowed from one of the other professors at my father's college. Before it was dark, we walked the trails and picked up branches. My father told me to look for ones that were just brown. I still remember carefully examining to be sure there wasn't a speck of green. He used those branches to build us a little campfire each night. It's funny thinking back on that. I wonder how my father learned to build a campfire—it seems so out of character for him—sleeping in the woods, hiking, building a campfire."

"Maybe he was a Cub Scout," I say.

My mother smiles. "You could be right. I guess there's so much I don't know about him. He didn't make it easy."

"Are we going back there, to your hometown on this trip? Maybe you could find out more about your father."

The restaurant grows quiet. The noisy family beside us is gone, leaving only sprinkles of sand on the blue floor tiles and crumbled white napkins on the table. The men behind us are eating now, and I hear a muted snap as one of them cracks a king crab leg. The flow of new diners shuffling across the floor has stopped.

"Well, Anna Lee. I suppose that would be quite impossible now. And no. We're not going back there. I'm never going back."

"Maybe your father's cousin could help you find out more about him? Would she know more about his childhood?"

She holds up one of her hands in front of her, palm facing me. At first, I think she's trying to quiet me, but then I realize she's studying her manicure. She moves to the other hand before tilting her head to the side, her eyes narrowing.

"I suppose. Maybe she remembers *some* things."

Nell pushes through the swinging door at the back of the dining room.

"Maybe some things," she continues. "But one day I'll know everything, one day before long…"

There's a look on her face that's unfamiliar. I want to ask her what she means by *one day*, but Nell is at the table, lifting the heavy white ceramic plates off the tray with one hand while balancing the tray with the other. She's placed the wrong order in front of the wrong diner, but I don't want to make the exchange in front of her.

"Anything else I can get for you ladies?"

My mother smiles and lifts her mug.

"Would you mind another refill when you have a chance?"

Chapter 21

My mother had one instruction for our accommodations that night—it must be oceanfront. Nell recommended The Pen Block Plantation.

"Sounds lovely," my mother said as we left our table.

Pen Block doesn't sound lovely, nor beachy. I expect to see a prison-like cement building, but as the resort comes into view it looks fine–a little dated, but fine. It's even better inside with fresh paint and modern, nautical seating and accessories that feel like a recent refresh. There's a hit of instant energy as I step into our room. One of the walls is painted ultramarine— my favorite shade of blue.

I'm still staring at the wall as my mother pulls open the slider to the balcony.

"Oh, Anna Lee. Come look!"

The view of the Atlantic is perfect. Not a view from the side. Not a view with another hotel right in the middle. There's nothing between us and the ocean. Not even ugly power lines.

"How long can we stay?"

My mother laughs. "We're only booked for the night, but we could always extend."

"I think we should extend," I say, stepping up on the foot-rest to settle back in one of the canvas-backed stools that could be found on a movie set with "Director" stitched on the back. "I could sit here all day."

The light is starting to fade, but not the surf. The whooshing in and out continues. I lean to the side, my head resting against the plastic pole that stretches the canvas. There's a slight breeze and an occasional mist. One section of sky is the same ultramarine as the accent wall in our room—close to a perfect match. I focus on the shifting shades of color, bands of brightness, darkness, and every hue in-between. I close my eyes and count the waves' ins and outs in pairs: 2, 4, 6, 8... Even with my eyes closed I see the color—it's mesmerizing. I sink deeper and deeper into the depths of ultramarine when I feel a soft touch on my arm. I open my eyes. There's barely any light left in the sky.

"You were sleeping, Anna Lee—I was afraid your neck would stiffen in that position."

I rub my neck and take a deep breath. "Probably not the best sleeping position," I admit. "It's peaceful out here."

"I think you're right about our stay," my mother says. "This is definitely a good spot to extend."

I nod and yawn.

"Do you have any energy left?" she asks. "Up for a walk on the beach?"

I hop down from the chair.

The halls and elevator are empty, and I wonder if we're the only guests of the resort until we're in the lobby. There's a group of senior citizens talking loudly while a young woman checks them in at the front desk. Six large wheeled carts hold stacks of luggage—some on the edge of sliding off. I count 11 suitcases on one–a mixture of hard, canvas, and duffle bags. Two of the cases have bright red ribbons on the handles, a technique my mother has used on flights to easily identify which blue roller bag belongs to her.

We step outside and the stars are starting to appear, shiny little pearls. Outdoor lights partially illuminate the long, narrow boardwalk over the sand. We walk closer to the sound of the surf, my mother's tiny braids falling in and out of shadow as she moves in front of me. I take a deep breath. I'm not angry. I'm not embarrassed. I'm not thinking of ways to end our time together. Wishing on a star isn't enough. I send up a prayer to remember this moment. Everything is where it should be. The smell of salt, the crescent moon, the quiet of early night.

Morning. I'm still in that peaceful place from last night and I strain for the sound of the surf beyond the thick sliding glass door. I hear the dull whirl of our bathroom fan, and I turn to confirm my mother is out of bed. It's only 6:25, so I close my eyes and drift back into my perfect place.

I'm opening my eyes again, feeling slightly groggy, like I've slept too long. But the whirling continues, so I must have closed my eyes for just a moment.

I get out of bed, push back the curtains, and open the slider. The sound is clear and instantly soothing. The thick grass between the hotel and the sand is a startling bright green with just a few brown palm strands littering the view. I hear a motor and turn to see the sand cleaner driving up the beach, pulling in clumped pockets of sand, seaweed, pebbles, and shells, leaving a new top layer of silky sand behind.

A few people walk along the water's edge, some bending down to pick up shells. From the distance, I see people turn the shells to study for imperfections. Most are tossed aside.

A woman walks down the boardwalk, balancing a beach chair and huge pink and white striped beach bag. Two young children follow. Maybe it's later than it seems. I check my cell phone, charging by the side of the bed. The time doesn't seem right—9:15. That would mean my mother has been in the bathroom three hours. I shake my head. She must have returned to bed and is now taking a shower. I'm surprised she didn't grab a cup of coffee first.

I think about Miss June's letters. About opening the next one in the stack. And then I envision reading her beautiful words on the balcony, only to have my mother interrupt. I pick up my phone instead, not expecting much. Does anyone my age have a more depressing social life?

I'm surprised to see texts from two friends—both wondering why I haven't texted them. I send back duplicate responses and pull out my journal and bright pink pencil case decorated with words in various fonts and colors: *Explore; Live your Life; Laugh; Dance; Smile More.* A gift from my mother. Inside are pre-sharpened pencils with varied geometric patterns. I pull out the most colorless so I won't get distracted—light gray swirls on a white background.

Back on the balcony, I think about my mother's vague comment yesterday: *But one day I'll know everything, one day before long...*

The gray swirls between my fingers, I add to my list of what makes my mother crazy:

#6 - *Talks in code.*

#7 - *Spends too much time in the bathroom.*

Evidence of my mother's altered mental capacity is growing. I hear the squeak of the bathroom door and turn. She's a shade lighter than the soft gray swirls on my pencil. She doesn't smile, call out *Anna Lee*, or even look in my direction. She sits on the side of the bed, head in her hands.

This is how she used to look. And how she used to *be*—every morning. Quiet. I can almost hear the rolling wine bottles in the recycle bin. There's a flash in my mind that maybe she drank last night. But it's not possible–we were together.

"Are you alright?" I ask quietly. "Can I get you anything?"

"Water. And coffee."

I get some water out of the bathroom sink. When she takes the cup, her hand is shaking. I fill another cup with water and pour it into the espresso machine to start the process. It begins its cycle and my mother moans, "So loud."

There's no way to quiet the machine unless I turn it off, so I let it continue. I'm already opening two small tubs of cream.

I exchange the water for her coffee—hands still shaking. She sips slowly, elegantly, like a woman at a fancy tea party, not a woman barely balancing on the edge of the bed.

I wait until she's finished before I ask.

"What's wrong?"

She hesitates just long enough for me to know she's grasping for an answer.

"Must have been the shrimp yesterday. I'm just so…unsettled."

"Can I get you something else?"

"No. I've been up most of the night. If you don't mind, I'd like to go back to sleep. Why don't you get ready for the beach? I'll find you later."

After protesting that she might need me, I change into my swimsuit in the bathroom, hoping she doesn't become "unsettled" again before I'm finished. When I return to the room, I can hear her heavy breathing—she's already asleep. I grab my beach bag, throw in a towel, lotion, sunglasses, book, my phone, and some money for breakfast and maybe lunch. Then I carefully remove a handful of Miss June's letters from the stack and place them inside my book so they won't get crumpled.

The sun streams across the lobby, and I stop at the coffee cart for a muffin and hot green tea. I balance everything, put my sunglasses on, then walk out the automatic doors.

A few groups are setting up residences for the day. Three elderly women, probably among those I saw in the lobby last night, are easing back into beach chairs.

Nearby, a handful of 30-something women are lining up chairs along the surf, adjusting to find just the right spot so they won't tilt in the unsteady sand, or get washed out with a big wave.

Two preschool-aged girls race around a wide green striped blanket as their mother pulls back and forth on the umbrella to dig it into the sand. She knocks her white baseball cap off in the process, and one of the girls snatches it and puts it on her own head, laughing while the older one chases her toward the surf. The girls are in the water, the waves hitting their ankles, their knees. The foam clinging to their legs. My chest suddenly feels tight. I want to tell the mother her daughters are in danger, but I can't speak, can't move—my feet stuck in the sand like it's cement.

Chapter 22

Everything around me is out of focus. I squint and see her—the mother running toward the surf and into the water. And now they're all walking back toward the green striped blanket, holding hands.

I close my eyes and my tightness eases. I decide to avoid all the groups and move to an empty section of the beach. At least empty for now. I know better than to think I'll have it all to myself for long.

The sun falls behind a cloud and the coolness washes over me, the hairs on my arms standing up like there's eminent danger. By the time I've spread out my beach towel and taken my first sip of tea, the sun has emerged once more. I start to think about my mother, then push her back into her own cloud—way in the back of my mind. It's just like her to try and spoil a beautiful beach day, but I have more pressing priorities to think about. What should I read first "The Glass Castle" or Miss June's letters?

The book's already making me feel better about my parents—the author's childhood is much, much crazier than mine. But the letters win from both the sentimental and reasoned side of my brain. I can read my book anytime, but I can only read the letters when my mother isn't around. Or at least, I'm not comfortable reading them in front of her.

The first two letters in the stack detail more about her life in the classroom. She's substituting for the art teacher now. Although she feels less qualified in that subject, she likes getting to work with all the students in the school. She describes a few of the art projects—plaster of Paris sculptures animals, watercolor paintings of the desert, carved pumpkins.

The next envelope reveals a card with a bright yellow sunflower on the front. Inside, she's added two photos. The first is of me in the white dress I remember from my father and Miss June's wedding day. On the back she's written *prettiest flower girl ever!* The second picture is of me and Miss June on a merry-go-round, side-by-side on white painted horses. I'm about 5 or 6. I flip it over, but there's nothing on the back. I stare hard at the scene and try to remember. Maybe my father was the photographer. The camera is zoomed in pretty tight on us. I can see the carved center column of the carousal and pieces of a few other horses, but nothing in the surrounding area. I'll have to ask Miss June when I visit her.

That last thought surprises me, but not completely. Of course I want to visit her. But even a phone call will mean I have to tell her what my mother did. How she kept those letters from me for all these years. Why did my mother always complicate everything?

I double check the letters and card to see if she's added a cell phone number. Not yet. I tuck the pictures back inside the envelope and back inside the book. My shoulders already feel warm, so I pull out my sunscreen from the beach bag and remember to apply a little extra to my shoulders and nose—areas prone to sunburn.

About five years ago, I spent part of my summer with painful reminders about the importance of sunscreen. Cool cloths applied to my back each night so I could sleep. Daily

Epsom salt baths. Gentle application of aloe each morning. Despite all that care, I blistered. When I returned to school, my skin was still flaking and I had to rub myself against the back of our classroom's pale-yellow plastic chairs to satisfy the itch.

From that point on, my mother reminded me about applying and reapplying sunscreen. She'd often pull out my sunscreen, shake it to make sure there was enough left for my next trip to the beach, then check the expiration date.

My mother could be obsessive about the slightest issues. After I helped our neighbor clear away weeds in the back of their yard, my mother spotted a tick crawling up my arm. It wasn't imbedded in my skin, but she immediately called the doctor. When the scheduler tried to push off the appointment until later in the week, my mother lied.

"I think there's a bullseye pattern on her skin. She could have Lyme's disease—she needs to be seen today."

As the conversation continued, I knew she'd get the appointment. My mother could wear down the most stubborn of people. When the doctor asked about the bullseye pattern, she pulled my arm toward her to take a closer look.

"Hmm, I could have sworn I saw a bullseye developing," she said. "That's strange. Really strange. Maybe it was a shadow."

Most the time she thought she knew more than the doctor, so she didn't even respond to questions.

One day when I was walking home from school, a couple of younger boys who lived down the street were looking at a spot on the ground.

"I think it's a beehive," one of them said as I walked up.

It looked like a clump of red clay with a hole in the middle.

"That's not a beehive," I laughed.

They didn't believe me.

"It's just a mound of dirt," I said, and slammed my foot on top to prove it.

There was a whirl of motion before the first sting. Then the second and third. I stopped counting after ten and just started running. The bees kept stinging.

My bottom lip, right cheek, and right wrist were already swollen. My mother made a quick paste of water and baking soda and applied to the stings with cotton balls. As soon as the last dab was on my wrist, she put her purse on her arm.

"Come on, Anna Lee, the doctor needs to see you."

By the time we were back in the examination room, the ice I was applying reduced the swelling to mere puffiness.

"I'm feeling better, really," I said, shifting my body slightly from one side to the other so I could hear the stiff white paper beneath me crackle. "Maybe we should leave."

My mother was pacing.

"I can't believe the doctor is taking so long," she said, her voice getting louder. "You were stung at least twenty times."

I hear some voices outside the little room and footsteps on the tile before the door opened.

"Oh, Dr. Owens," my mother said flushing a bit. "I didn't expect it to take so long for something so serious."

The doctor was flipping slowly through the papers on the clipboard.

"OK," he finally said, looking up. "Let's see what we have here."

There was near silence in the room for at least a minute as the doctor looked over my face and wrist. I tried to count the tongue depressors on the shelf, but they were bunched in the jar too tightly.

"Have you ever had an allergic reaction to bees?"

I shrugged my shoulders, so he turned to my mother.

"Has she?"

"She was stung at least twenty times."

He took a deep breath and let it out quickly.

"I understand, but has she had an allergic reaction in the past?"

"We've been waiting so long, I'm surprised she's not completely healed up by now."

The doctor frowned, then wrote something down on the paper attached to the clipboard.

"Are you in pain?"

"Not anymore…but I was. When it happened and after it happened."

"But not now?"

"A little, but not like before."

My mother crossed her arms firmly.

"Again. We've been waiting a long time."

I spent a few more uncomfortable moments in the small, stark-white room. Ultimately, the doctor took out his notepad from his pocket and wrote down two words: *Tylenol* and *Benadryl.*

"This should get you through the next 24-hours. You don't need to take the Benadryl unless you start swelling again."

On the ride home, my mother continued her rant about the wait time. She stopped at Lee's Pharmacy, a local place that also sold milk and eggs, and even rented DVDs.

"You don't need to get the Benadryl," I called out the window, after she insisted I rest in the car. "He said I might not need it."

"Anna Lee—you had at least twenty stings! I'm getting the Benadryl."

I don't think we ever opened the bottle. For all I know it's still sitting in the back of the cabinet, topped with a layer of dust and long past the expiration date.

There was one thing that still lingered from that episode. I was afraid of bees. I didn't care how ridiculous I looked when a bee flew in my direction, I moved out of the way no matter how inconvenient the location—at school, in a restaurant, and once on a date with Sean. It was almost dark and we were playing miniature golf by the pier. I felt a sting. I expected a mosquito bite, but when I turned, the bee was still lingering by its prey. I threw down my golf club and tripped on the ledge that bordered the third hole, the one with the windmill.

It was funny. Funny then. Funny now. I'm holding back a laugh thinking about it and there she is—my mother is finally up and out.

"Are you feeling better?" I ask as she sets her beach bag on the sand.

"I'm feeling better enough to have this," she says, holding up her super-sized cardboard coffee cup like she's making a toast.

The sun slips behind a cloud and the temperature drops. I pull my old tie-dye t-shirt out of my bag.

"Oh, Anna Lee," she says, less spirited than usual. "You still have it. Do you remember that day?"

"Oh, yes," I say laughing. "I thought our hands would be permanently stained. The fuchsia was especially hard to wash off."

"My nails were a combination of gold and purple for weeks."

My tenth birthday. My mother and her friends Latrice and Edna came up with a 70's themed party—not surprising since they all dressed like hippies, or at least bohemians. The unsuspecting parents dropped their girls off for ice cream and cake. When they arrived to pick them up, the girls carried their still dripping shirts in plastic grocery store bags. The dye on the shirt was contained, but the bold colors, at least two dozen different hues, had settled on skin, hair, shoes, and clothing.

I could tell that the parents were angry. In truth, it was just the mothers. The two fathers who arrived didn't seem to notice.

One girl from my class Tina, a tiny, quiet girl from Guatemala with brown eyes peeking out under thick bangs, had pink dye on her teeth. Tina smiled when her mother arrived. Her English was limited, and my mother's attempts to explain failed. When Tina returned to school after the weekend, I could still see a tinge of pink on her two front teeth.

Most of the girls were happy with the shirts, despite the extra dye. Sophie said her mother made her throw it away. When two of the girls from the party wore their shirts to school one day, Sophie cried.

The sun was nesting behind some new, thick clouds, but I leave the shirt on and settle back with my book. I was embarrassed by my mother's efforts at the time, but now it's a nice, funny memory.

I can hear my mother's loud breathing again—she's asleep. I wonder if she applied lotion before she came down. The sun is reflecting on half of her face since her hat is tilted off to one side. I gently adjust it so she's fully shaded, expecting her to wake up, but she doesn't. It's been a long time since she's slept so soundly.

Chapter 23

My mother's ready for a late afternoon coffee, a sign she's feeling better. She has her recommendation—The Fractured Prune. An image of an actual fractured prune appears in my head as we drive, the windows down and the air blowing our hair.

Would the prune be chopped in two? No, then it would be called The Broken Prune. Maybe crushed? No, that would be The Mashed Prune.

My mother's playing some local music now—one of at least three bands from Jersey she follows. Sounds like it was recorded live, probably at our church's weekly coffee house.

Life has never known so true
Life has never been for you
So true, for you
Life has never been for you

A song with lyrics as confusing as The Fractured Prune. Maybe neither the place nor the song are supposed to make sense. Or maybe I just think too long and too hard about everything in life instead of just experiencing it. My mother starts singing and I join her. The beginning of a new philosophy—less thinking, more experiencing.

Forever lasts just one day
Forever blue, forever you

My ban on overthinking lasts about a minute. I'm back to wondering—was the songwriter more focused on making sure the words rhymed rather than telling a story? She's still singing when we arrive at The Fractured Prune.

Two things I notice quickly: it smells amazing; and there are no prune donuts on the menu board. I think this "experiencing life" is going to take more practice.

"Hmmm, might take us some time," my mother says to the cashier. "Don't you think, Anna Lee?"

"It's overwhelming."

There are 17 favorite donuts listed on the big white sign. I read through the list a couple times, but keep going back to the Banana Cream Pie, Strawberry Shortcake, and S'more. In fairness, one of the favorites is called Ms. Prunella, which has a mixed berry glaze and cinnamon sugar—but still no actual prunes.

As if 17 choices aren't enough, we can create our own by choosing a glaze and a toping. I already know my mother will insist on making her own before she tells me.

"Create your own? Oh, how fun, Anna Lee! Definitely the Key Lime glaze," she says, pausing to take a sip of her coffee. "What works with that?"

I read through the toppings.

"Shredded coconut…graham crackers?"

"Oh yes! Is it possible to do both?"

The cashier nods. "We can do that. And, something for you?" she asks looking at me.

"I'm thinking the S'more…or is the Banana Cream Pie better?"

"They're all good," she says, pausing. "My favorite is actually the Strawberry Shortcake."

"That was my other choice—let's go with that."

We wait inside until our order is ready, and I feel the warm donut through the thin paper plate. There's no seating inside, so we step outside to an empty bench.

We're both biting in and there's no sound—our teeth sinking into dough. I expect my mother to make some big proclamation about how good the donuts are, but she's too focused on eating. Before I realize it, I'm taking my last bite, and even roll my plate to tilt the crumbs into my mouth.

My mother is still swallowing the last bits. There's a piece of coconut in the corner of her mouth and she uses her tongue to pull it inside. *Good to the last drop.* She says that a lot, but only when she's finishing a cup of coffee. She once told me the phrase was from an old commercial, one she remembered from her childhood.

"Don't you think we need to get another one?" she asks.

"For later?"

"For now, later, whenever you want it. Why don't you get a Banana Cream *and* a S'more?"

"Are we staying at the hotel tonight?" I ask, suddenly wondering if we've missed checkout time.

"Already taken care of," she says.

As we walk back to the counter, I'm thinking of eating a Fractured Prune donut tonight on the balcony, counting the whooshing ins and outs in pairs, the stars forming overhead in a darkening aquamarine sky.

We order pizza for dinner. Neither of us are ready to leave that balcony view, and the coffee pods for the espresso machine have been refilled so my mother's fix is easily satisfied.

There's a slight breeze on the patio—not so strong that our napkins are blowing off the table, but enough to carry the salty mist of the ocean. My mother is pulling off another slice of pizza from the box, struggling because the pieces aren't cleanly cut.

"Are you sure you're not overdoing it?" I ask.

"Oh, Anna Lee—this is only my second piece," she laughs.

"But you had two donuts earlier, and you were so sick this morning. You said you were *unsettled*."

Her lips tighten, and she looks away, taking a first bite from the new slice. Chewing, swallowing. Thinking about a response.

"I suppose I'm pretty lucky."

"How's that?"

"I'm not usually sick for long."

She's taking another bite, and I'm counting the waves. Trying to stay focused on the experience so I won't consider what she's *not* saying.

"I think I've trained my body," she continues. "A single Mom has to do that. There were times when we were both sick and you were too young to take care of yourself. I willed my body to recover fast, so I could help you get better."

"Like that time we both had the flu?"

"Exactly, Anna Lee. What grade were you in? Third?"

"It was fourth—I remember because I had Miss Sylvia that year."

"Miss Sylvia! She was wonderful, even dropping off homework at the house."

"And risking catching the flu herself," I say.

"Well, teachers don't get many breaks during the school year. Maybe she was *hoping* she'd get the flu."

We laugh and my mother looks relieved that we've moved off the original topic. Relieved that she doesn't have to tell me the truth. Again.

We have an uneventful second day at Pen Block. It's a bit cooler and cloudier, but still beach-worthy weather. My mother runs off to make a few calls, so I send and receive a few texts from friends and read the next chapters of my book.

Our second night at the hotel started with a short walk to a beachy restaurant that specialized in fresh fish and had an extensive salad bar that took up an entire room. My mother ordered us two virgin Strawberry Daiquiris. She didn't ask me first—but I didn't refuse it.

We're now walking back to the hotel along the beach in the thinnest of light. I step into the surf by accident, my breath instantly drawing in, but my mother puts her hand on my back and moves me up to the sand, taking my hand. I'm not sure if she's holding my hand for her benefit, because she can't see well in the moonlight, or if it's a gesture to keep me close.

She already had a cup of coffee at the end of the meal, which arrived with her coconut cream pie. But inside the lobby she can't resist pouring herself one more cup—half from the regular pot and half from the decaf. This is something new.

Back upstairs, we sit on the balcony while she drinks her coffee—not talking, just listening to the waves. There's a strangeness about it all, and I wonder if she has some new secret she's waiting to reveal. But once she finishes her coffee, she yawns and steps down from the chair.

"I'm gonna call it a night, Anna Lee. We can take our time in the morning, check out isn't 'til noon."

I'm still counting the ins and outs when the light goes off in the room. I know if I stay on the balcony any longer,

I'll probably fall asleep, and I do, but not for long. I slide the balcony door slowly, quietly so I won't wake her up and feel for my t-shirt on the end of the bed before going in the bathroom to change.

My mother left her small travel bag on the counter. Unusual because she always likes to keep everything out of the way when we travel. I put on the bathroom fan and unzip the bag. I know it's wrong, an invasion of her privacy. And there's a slight feeling of dread. Not because there is any chance of getting caught, but because there may be something inside that I won't be able to ignore.

On top is a large, clear plastic bag. There are about a half-dozen prescription medications inside. I return the bag back quickly, zip the case, and sit down on the toilet lid. I wipe my wet palms on my shorts and count the fan cycles for a few minutes, until my heart stops racing.

My mother is addicted to prescription medicine. She wasn't "unsettled" from the shrimp dinner. She probably took too many pills.

When I step out of the room she's breathing loudly, rhythmically. I lay in the next bed listening to her sleep, knowing I'll probably be awake all night.

Chapter 24

We're packing up and my mother is her usual chatty self. No sign that she's high.

"I've already talked with Sylvia down at the front desk," she says. "We're just a couple hours from Myrtle Beach. I've always wanted to go there."

"Hmmm."

"Sylvia's son lives there. She even called him and asked about coffee shops."

"Coffee shops, really? Did you even ask about a place to stay?"

"He recommended so many coffee shops and restaurants that Sylvia had to write them all down."

"But no recommendations on a hotel?" I ask again.

"She mentioned one, maybe I wrote it down," she says, zippering her large bag, not the one with the drugs. "It's the off season—we'll find something."

I'm staring at the ultramarine wall, sitting on my luggage to force it shut, and quickly pulling the zipper around before it pops open. The addition of Miss June's box of letters makes it hard to close.

"How long is the drive?"

"Were you listening, Anna Lee? It's about two hours."

Two hours next to my mother not talking about her drug issues. Since I'd forgotten to charge my phone last night, I'd have to hope my aging battery would hold on or find something to count along the way to distract me. Motorcycles? Red cars? Signs with the word *Beach*? Yes—signs with the word beach. Certainly enough to keep me occupied.

As we cross the lobby, my mother gives a quick wave to the woman behind the counter who is pointing out something on a map to a hotel guest.

"That's Sylvia—I won't bother her. She's so sweet. Even gave me her cell phone number in case we had questions."

I wonder if Sylvia knows that my mother is crazy. And addicted to narcotics. As we wheel our bags toward the door, my mother stops and holds her index finger up to indicate she'll be right back. She turns sharply then heads straight to the coffee station.

Could crazy be contagious? My fears seem intense, my dreams confusing, my future hopeless. All worse since we started this trip.

My mother's walking toward the Jeep, bag over her shoulder, pulling her luggage behind her. In the other hand, she carries her coffee, swinging it briskly. She doesn't need to leave breadcrumbs. There's probably a long thin line of brown dribbles from the lobby to our parking spot.

Before we put our bags in the back, we open the doors to let in some fresh air. The heat inside must be percolating all the spilled coffee–the smell is stronger than usual.

I won't want to admit it to my mother, but I'm looking forward to Myrtle Beach. My friend Tanni and her family spent a week there each summer and she said everything was way better and bigger than our little beach at home. Really, our little beach didn't present much in the way of competition.

One actual sit-down restaurant. A rundown bar that also sold bait. An ice cream stand that occasionally offered more than chocolate, vanilla, and strawberry. And no coffee shop. But there was a tattoo parlor and a tax preparer. My mother was always trying to figure out a way to get a coffee shop close to home. She told me often. She also told Jim Monroe, the tax man.

"Jim doesn't need to be open during the summer months. I told him he could save some money on rent. I wish someone would strike a deal with him—he could use the store from January through April. It's just the right size to be a coffee shop the rest of the year. And why does the tattoo parlor need to be by the beach? There'd have more clients if they moved over to Central Avenue."

And on, and on, and on she'd go. Her ideas certainly did make sense, even if they were fueled by her addiction. The only time the tax guy's parking lot was filled was January through April. And Central Avenue would be a much better spot for customers looking for ink. Our town didn't have much in the way of an art scene, but what little we had was on that main street—a small art gallery, bookstore, and a tiny artists' co-op with mostly jewelry, and a few paintings on commission.

My mother has enough problems of her own. I wonder why she's always trying to solve others? There are the problems I know she has, and the problems she's probably going to share with me once we get to the next hotel. My heart's pounding, so I start counting.

I'm seeing more billboards than I expect. With the most recent sign, *Carolina Beach Rentals,* my count is up to eight. *Retro Beach Plumbers,* featuring a sullen-looking white-haired lady in a periwinkle housedress holding a plunger in the air, is my favorite so far.

My mother is occupied with her music. Singing each song so loudly that I can barely hear the actual singer. I'm not sure I noticed it before, but now that I know about her part-time singing career, I realize she really does have a nice voice. At least she's not in a mood to talk. I'm afraid she'll say something, anything really, that annoys me, and I'll tell her I know about the pills. As if on cue, the next billboard reads: *Suffer no more! Beachside Pain Clinic—walk-ins welcome!* I glance at my mother to see if she notices, but she's staring straight ahead, making whiny sounds to mimic the guitar lead in the song.

There's a string of signs all advertising Oceanside Beach Resort. There are different photos on each—a couple in a fancy restaurant, chairs lined up in the sand, two little girls playing with a beach ball in the pool. But each ad includes the Oceanside Beach Resort name and address on the bottom. Thanks to the resort, my count is up to a dozen.

I see a group of ads coming up and I'm hopeful. In the distance, I can see swirls of waves around the border, a look that reminds me of van Gogh's Starry Night with the words: *Sunny Daze Swim Shoppe.* But no *beach.* These signs are packed in closely and I scour each one quickly, trying to add to my total.

Fairfield Insurance: Auto, Home, Life.
Regional Hospital Center
24-hour Emergency Room

Feeling hot, hot, hot?
Right Now Cooling Services

And, the final disappointment.

Don't Drink and Drive

Disappointing AND ironic.

I tuck my current count of 12 in the back of my mind and start to count mile markers. Much more fruitful. I'm up to ten markers before we reach the next billboard.

Beach Rentals and Sales

Thirteen!

"Anna Lee—did you fall asleep?"

I'm so focused on finding another *beach* that I forget she's right beside me, until she shouts.

"No. Just thinking."

"Well, while you're thinking could you also check the map on your phone? Are we still headed the right way?"

I'm pulling up my app. "Umm, yeah—still good."

"How much longer?" she asks, sounding annoyed.

"You're the one who wanted to go on this road trip. And forced me to go."

"Forced you? Is that really what you think?"

I decide to avoid conflict as usual. "We're half-way there."

Half-way to learning another secret. I wonder if there was a bus that would take me back home.

I'm hoping for more signs to count along the way, but hoping even more that she doesn't start a conversation. My first wish is granted. Two more signs–both with my word. I glance at my mother and she opens her mouth. Here comes another revelation, another unwanted surprise. And then she starts to sing.

I immediately see why Tanni likes Myrtle Beach—she's right about bigger and better. Along the main road, there are restaurants, hotels, condos, stores, and signs for even more places nearby. I'm wishing we'd driven straight past Hanover—Pennsylvania or Maryland. And straight past Deep Creek, Alexandria, Virginia Beach, and Wilmington. I look at my cell phone to send Tanni a message, but then I remember. She's out of the U.S. without an international calling plan. At least we'll have a lot to talk about when I return. Whenever that is.

Even though I'm enjoying the silence, I'm anxious to explore.

"What's the name of the place Sylvia suggested?" I ask.

"Oh–something with Reef in the name."

I'm opening my app, typing in *Reef Myrtle Beach*.

"Could it be Tropical Reef Hotel?"

"Any other Reefs?"

"That's it. And, it's not far. It's on North Ocean Boulevard. Is that the road we're on now?"

"I think so. Let's find a road sign," my mother says, shifting her head from side to side.

I catch a view of the beach between buildings. And silently plead the place is on the ocean, or at least a short walk to the beach.

"Yes," my mother says, pointing to the street sign. "We're on the right road. Just keep an eye out for the hotel."

The hotels on the oceanfront are lined up neatly, like properly postured subjects in front of their king, Ra—god of the sun. The smaller human subjects are probably already lined up in their beach chairs.

On the other side of the road, I only see parking lots, retail, and restaurants, so I shift all my attention to the ocean side. We're almost on top of it before I see the sign.

"Right there," I point, and my mother does a wide turn into the driveway that takes us to the main entrance.

"How about I leave you here with the suitcases while I find a place to park?"

Inside the lobby, there's a fresh scent that's familiar. It's not the smell of the ocean exactly. I wonder if all beach resorts have the same artificial scent pulsing through their air filtering systems. I can't smell the coffee, but I see it on the other side of the lobby. Will my mother's first stop be there or the front desk? Before I have a chance to guess, I see her. She's checking us in.

There's a sign with an arrow for Amour Café. It's almost 2:00 and we haven't eaten lunch yet—I'm glad we won't have to go far.

My mother passes me on her way to the coffee station and she pumps from two different carafes. That half-caf thing again.

"Alright Anna Lee, we're heading to the 16th floor."

We pull our luggage into the elevator and she virtually bursts with excitement when the door closes.

"There's an outdoor oceanfront pool, an indoor lazy river, and hot tubs! Are we changing into our suits?"

"Are we going to eat lunch? I know you're fine with coffee, but other people get hungry."

She ignores my snark. "Amour Café, Anna Lee—right here at the hotel. We'll eat first, then decide between the pool area and the beach."

The room features four complementary shades of blue and the view really delivers Tanni's "bigger and better" Myrtle Beach slogan. I thought we'd be too far up to hear the surf, but the familiar ins and outs sail right up to our 16th floor balcony.

We change and are out the door quickly with our beach bags. My mother's wearing her most obnoxiously bright coverup. With large yellow sunflowers, at least it's a departure from her signature red and pink.

The Café offers indoor and outdoor tables and we're seated in the sunshine with menus and glasses of ice waters. Only one other table is occupied—a young couple holding hands across the top of the table. There's the thinnest of breezes carrying salt from the ocean.

"I have a good feeling about Myrtle Beach," my mother says. "I booked two nights here."

Tanni and her family always stayed for a full week, but at least two nights are better than one. We started out with single nights, and now we're up to two. Maybe we'll stay three nights at the next place. Or maybe there won't be a next place. Nice thought, but I can't raise enough optimism to believe that's true.

I can tell my mother likes the restaurant. She orders a coffee with her sandwich and they leave the whole pot on the table. The waitress mentions the "famous breakfast buffet," but I know the pot of coffee will be enough to draw us back for breakfast.

It's already after 3:00 when we walk down onto the sand, our feet sinking with each step. We edge closer to the water. I'm carrying my purple and teal flip flops and drop one of them as I step down into a small hole in the sand. Just like that, it's floating away and all I can do is stand there. I can't take a step toward it. Not one.

My mother is running into the low surf, her cover-up soaked and clinging to her body. My flip flop is just a wave away. She steps over the wave, but it's still out of reach. Cool water laps over my feet and I'm sweating. The haze of the sun is so bright I can't focus or even count the ins and outs. Where's my mother? I finally see her as she's standing right in front of me, holding my flip flop. I just stare, my mouth dry, my hands motionless to take my escaped shoe.

"It's okay, Anna Lee," my mother says, taking my hand. "I'm here. I'm right here."

She pulls me close against her. The scent of her lilac perfume, which is usually too heavy for me, helps me breathe, so I inhale, exhale until my vision clears. I put my head on her shoulder as we walk up the beach, still barefoot as we reach the path to the hotel. My mother leans down to help guide my flip flops onto my feet. Then she hugs me close and whispers.

"There's something I need to tell you. Let's go back to our room."

Chapter 25

I quietly follow her, holding her hand and my head starts to clear. Why does she think this is the right moment to tell me about her issues with drugs?

The air hits my face as we step out on the balcony. We're side-by-side on lounge chairs, our feet stretched out before us—mine still wearing flip flops. I tilt my right foot to study the teal stripe on the side, and then the left. Two stripes on each. There are coral stripes on our thick cushions on our seats, and I start to count them until my mother interrupts.

"It's time I told you something. It's long-past time, really and I don't want to wait any longer."

I keep my eyes focused straight ahead on the ocean, the tips of the waves shining like the stiff, white icing peaks on the cupcakes from the bakery section of our town's grocery store.

"There's a reason you're afraid of the ocean."

Why was she making this conversation about me?

"Your fear of the ocean, it's my fault. You weren't always afraid."

Afraid. The word is too big for me. I feel uncomfortable, anxious when I cross from the sand to the water.

"Do you remember, Anna Lee?"

"Do I remember what?"

"The day on the beach when you became afraid?"

"I don't think I became afraid. I'm just careful."

My mother sighs and twists her hands and when she stops, I see them shake slightly. She's overdue for a coffee. Or maybe meds.

"No, Anna Lee. There's a real fear. Around the ocean and even in a pool when you try to put your face in the water."

"I like to swim."

"The backstroke, Anna Lee. Always the backstroke."

She's right. But that doesn't mean—

"You were eleven-years-old, Anna Lee. Just eleven."

"I could swim at eleven," I say, shaking my head.

"Yes," my mother said slowly. "You could swim. You could swim well. But not in a riptide."

"That's when the lifeguard calls everyone back."

"Yes, that's true now. But our beach didn't have lifeguards then."

"Really? When did that change?"

"The next summer, the summer after the riptide."

"So, there was a riptide and everyone realized we needed lifeguards?"

My mother takes a breath.

"I'll get to that. But let's start on July 15th."

"You remember the date?"

She takes another breath, this one deeper as she lifts her sunglasses just enough to wipe her eyes.

"Forever. It's a hard date to remember, but it's an important date to remember. It's important for a lot of reasons."

"Because we had a riptide and now we have lifeguards?"

My mother is wringing her hands again. "Just let me…"

"Do you want me to make you a coffee?"

"I do, but I want to tell you this first. Before I change my mind."

The breeze has evaporated, and I lean toward her. Suddenly, I don't want her to change her mind either.

"Do you remember anything about that day, Anna Lee?"

I shake my head.

"It actually started out to be a non-beach day. The forecast called for severe thunderstorms, and we'd had a hurricane pass through the previous two days," she says, looking out across the beach. "But just before noon, all the clouds were gone. As I was going into my bedroom to change, you came out of your bedroom with your suit on. We laughed because neither of us had said anything."

My mother and I did visit the beach a lot. But at some point that changed. At some point I stopped going as often. And I stopped going with my mother—at least most of the time.

"I made some quick sandwiches, threw them into the cooler..."

A strong breeze suddenly picks up, and I watch a bright pink and white striped umbrella roll down the beach.

"There was something else in the cooler," she says.

My mother pauses for some time. Quite a long time.

"Are you expecting me to guess what was in the cooler? Water, iced tea..."

"I don't want you to guess—it was wine. I'd already had a couple of glasses earlier, so I poured the rest into a thermos. It was—a large bottle. One that you'd serve at a party. I actually filled two thermoses."

I'm still staring at the umbrella, but it's stopped now. Several yards up the beach.

"I told you I drank, but I didn't tell you how much. And how often. But I need to finish. About July 15th."

There's a man in a black baseball cap running toward the umbrella. He's leaning forward, trying to run faster, but his feet are slowed by the sand.

"It turned out to be hotter than I expected at the beach. I didn't pack any water, and I was feeling dehydrated, so I told myself that wine was as good as water. I just needed to get it down quickly, and I did."

Her voice quiets at the end, but we're so close I hear her. *And I did.*

Even quieter, "I'd also had a couple of glasses earlier."

And then, she got in the car. And I got in the car. All those lectures from her about not drinking and driving. And she drove us to the beach. I want to point this out to her, but decide to let her finish.

"I thought the earlier weather would keep everyone away. It wasn't as crowded as a typical Saturday, but there were at least a dozen people there. Maybe a few more. Two kids building a sandcastle that looked more like an igloo. A couple of kids that you knew from school."

"How do you remember?"

"I told you. I remember. That day, I remember," she says. "Our previous neighbor Bonnie Simon was there, and she introduced us to her cousin Cindy who was visiting from Michigan. Someone I didn't know had an old umbrella set up near the grass, and it kept falling over. There was a teenaged boy who kept paddling out pretty far, then body surfing in—on one of those blow-up pool floats."

An image flashes and my head starts to hurt. It's hazy, but I can just picture an ultramarine float moving closer and closer toward me, rocking on the waves. And suddenly I'm reaching out.

Chapter 26

"Was it an ultramarine float?"

My mother frowns.

"Well, it was blue..."

A puffy, aquamarine float with a long body and a thicker horizontal section across the top to resemble a pillow. Parts of the float feel warm, other parts cool where water pooled in the ridges. A stiff white valve on the corner that scratched my leg. How do I remember that? Why do I remember that?

"Who was he—the boy on the float?" I ask.

"I think he was with the people under that old umbrella—the people we didn't know. I wish I'd asked his name."

My mother's hands are folded—still shaking. I put my hand on top with some pressure and she looks up at me, her eyes narrow like she's going to cry. I can feel her pulse and start counting the beats.

"You were in the water with your friends. The sun was pretty hot at this point, and I was drowsy..."

"From the wine?"

She pauses, then nods.

"I fell asleep on the blanket and then I heard someone shouting," she says, her eyes looking up like she's watching each moment of July 15th.

"People were moving toward the water, pointing. I got up and moved toward everyone else. My vision was blurred, but I saw someone out pretty far in the water, bobbing up and down. When my vision finally cleared I saw a flash of purple. I knew it was you."

"My purple swimsuit."

"I'd like to say I knew what to do—I'm your mother. But I didn't. I could barely move, my head was still clogged, my body unsteady from drinking. But he knew what to do. A complete stranger saved you, but not your mother."

"The boy on the float?"

She nods.

"Bonnie offered to drive us home. I never knew if she realized I'd been drinking, or was just too panicked to get behind the wheel. We didn't find out until the next day that you were caught in a riptide."

"You can't swim back straight—that's probably what I tried to do."

"I signed you up for a swim class that taught survival skills at the rec center the next month. That's where you learned about riptides. And I started a petition to get lifeguards on the beach. They were in place by the next summer."

"Is that when you stopped drinking?"

My mother pauses for so long, I wonder if she's weighing the value between telling me the truth or a lie. She finally looks directly at me.

"That day is the reason I stopped. I'm ashamed to say it didn't happen immediately. That night, after you were asleep, I opened another bottle. But I called Edna that night crying. Told her I couldn't stop. Told her my greatest fear was that your father would take you away from me. And then told her my second greatest fear was that your father *wouldn't* take you away from me.

"Edna came in the morning. She took my car keys and my wallet. She went through my cabinets and took all the wine. I even told her about the two bottles in my bedroom closet, and she took those too. She came back a couple hours later and told me she'd made some calls, told me to pack a bag for a couple of weeks."

My mother rubs her hands together, then folds them on her lap.

"I'm going to finish the story, Anna Lee. But would you mind making me that cup of coffee?"

It's not a humorous moment, but it's typical so I laugh. There's still the comfort of coffee, even when my mother is sharing her deepest, most shameful secret.

She follows me inside and sits on the bed while I fill the cardboard cup with water from the bathroom sink.

"I was still resisting. Said I couldn't leave you for a couple of weeks. That night, Edna called in reinforcements. Just the sight of my friends in our living room, knowing you were right there in your bedroom, I agreed. Before I changed my mind, I called your father, told him I needed a medical procedure, and there'd be some recovery time."

"He didn't ask what kind of procedure?"

My mother smiles.

"I used a tone that made your father think it was a *female procedure*. I knew he wouldn't ask."

I laugh. "I bet he was uncomfortable just thinking about it. Once, I forgot to pack my tampons and called him at work to see if he'd pick up a box on the way home. He asked if one of my friends could bring me some. I reminded him I was only 14 and none of my friends could drive. Then he asked if there was a delivery service I could call. I still remember how red his face was when he came home and handed me the bag."

"Yes, that's definitely your father!"

The coffee has finished its cycle and I'm opening one of those powered cream packets my mother hates.

"Oh wait, Anna Lee! I have some better creamer in my purse."

I realize we left the sliders open to the balcony.

"Do you want to sit back outside?"

"No—let's stay inside, if that's good with you. But leave the door open so we can hear the ocean."

I hand my mother her coffee and move the desk chair close to the bed.

She takes a long drink, tilts her head back and closes her eyes. Maybe her ritual is a form of absolution.

"That's good. Where did I stop? Oh—you stayed with your father."

"Where did you go?"

"It was about an hour away. First the detox. Physically brutal. Then moved into recovery. Emotionally brutal. That was the hardest time of my life. I didn't realize how much I relied on alcohol. It was a cure for everything bad in my life, a celebration for everything good. There were so many things I had to face. I could have lost you—that was the hardest. Also had to admit that my father's failings were my failings, too. I tried to hide from that one."

"What about your father? Were you able to forgive him? Did you think about calling him?"

"I forgave him, Anna Lee. But I still didn't want to see him. Even though I really did understand how hard it all was."

She takes another big sip and tilts her head back, like she's trying to remember everything that happened.

"I was all-in at this point," she continues. "So all-in that I realized I needed more time. I called your father and told him

I was still having some medical issues and you'd need to stay with him another week."

"What about your job?"

"Edna took care of that. She knew the editor, told him the same story about a procedure, and he didn't ask questions either. When I came home, there was a card in the mail that was signed by the rest of the staff. *Get well soon.* Still appropriate."

My mother answers all of my questions over the next hour. No relapses, but still not easy. As I expected, those church meetings were AA meetings and she still attends them. That's where she picked up a replacement addiction—coffee. The longest she's gone between meetings was a month and quickly realized that was a mistake.

The day she had the accident, she decided to go to an AA meeting, not the coffee shop like she told me. She never made it. It's been nearly two weeks since she's been to a meeting. She already looked up the meeting schedule in Myrtle Beach and is going to a nearby church tomorrow at lunchtime.

"The hardest part of it all and still the hardest part of it all, is knowing that my addiction almost cost your life. It's the most shameful thing I've ever done. That's why I can't drink again. Each time you panic when we're walking on the beach and you step into the water, each time you put your face in the water and that terrified look flashes. It's all a reminder. A reminder of what I did, and a reminder of what's at stake if I drink again."

She's still tempted, especially when she smells wine or even grapes—which is why she doesn't eat them. Our church uses grape juice, not wine for communion, but the taste of the grapes still lingers in her mouth. Probably why she's the first in line for coffee after the service.

"I started in college–telling myself that blacking out helped me forget," she said, shaking her head slightly. "But

I didn't forget for long. I just hated myself because I was just like the man I hated."

"Did you ever try to quit?"

"For a long time, I thought I could just cut back. I played these games with myself. Just two glasses now. One bottle for the weekend. I told myself I could have as much as I wanted *just this one time.*"

She eventually told my father, long after she was sober.

"He actually asked me if there was anything he could do—anything he could do to help me. Somehow I managed to quit while I was pregnant with you. It didn't stick after."

There's one question I don't ask her. What about the pills? The sound of the waves grows louder. From the room, I can see them crashing as a large white cargo ship passes further out to sea.

My question will have to wait for another day.

Chapter 27

The sun is various tones of orange, yellow, and red. I'm happy to be awake as it lifts over the ocean, like a child's brightly colored beach ball has been set aloft by the riptide equivalent for wind—rising higher, higher until it makes a hard stop, then escapes from view for a moment behind one lone cloud. But the cloud is too thin to hold it—the light filtering out in sharp diagonal rays.

I hear my mother move from the bed into the bathroom, and realize the light probably woke her since the curtains are wide open.

Last night, my mother decided to find a meeting after our talk. She looked tired, more tired than I've seen her in a while, but when she returned, her face was brighter. We took a long walk on the beach, and I skimmed the edge of the water, even letting the surf cover my feet. The light was low, but we saw a restaurant with a big balcony that faced the beach, so we kept walking toward it.

From our outside table, several spotlights brightened enough of the ocean for us to see the water's edge. There were a few filled tables around us on the balcony, but conversations were muted. Mostly I just heard the waves. My mother looked out across the beach and didn't look at me when she spoke.

"Maybe the ocean will be your friend again, Anna Lee."

I paused for a moment, not sure what to say at first. "Maybe."

Not really a promise, but not a rejection either.

After dinner, we walked back along the road—the head-lights from the cars casting shadows as they pass, palm trees illuminated with tiny white lights wrapped around the trunks, and groups of fireflies dancing in front of us.

"I don't think I've ever seen fireflies so late in the season," my mother said. "It's magical."

The dark sky was the richest shade of blue I ever saw—the stars highlighted its color. My mother took my hand in hers, so warm it transferred quickly to my own. I realized I was smiling.

My mother started to read signs—business advertise-ments, hotel names, street names. I joined in and we alternated, adding inflections and accents until we were laughing too hard to continue.

As we walked toward the lobby entrance, my mother stopped.

"I don't want this night to end," she said. "I was filled with dread for so long about telling you, and now this is my favorite night."

We sat outside on the balcony, mostly quiet. The waves sounded almost fragile as they reached across the sand toward us.

My mother never went inside to make an evening cup of coffee.

This morning, with the sun streaming into our room, she's practically power walking to the coffee maker, water already in hand to fill the machine.

"I hope you slept well, Anna Lee! You fell asleep last night on the balcony. So peaceful. I hated to wake you up."

I don't remember. "I slept well, just surprised to wake so early."

"Looks like a perfect beach day. Maybe you didn't want to waste any of it."

The coffee is sputtering as it starts to brew and a thin burst of steam escapes the top. A chimney releasing a first puff of smoke.

"Want me to make one for you too?

"What are we doing for breakfast?"

"Downstairs?"

"The buffet?" I ask. "I'm not sure I can eat that much for breakfast, and it's probably pretty expensive."

"Don't worry about that, Anna Lee. Eat what you like. Don't feel like you have to get your money's worth," she smiles.

The money. I'd almost forgotten. How was she funding this trip? She'd always been so…*restrained* with her money. Although maybe it was her many years of restraint that allowed her to save for the trip. Doubtful. Everyone knew our local Gazette didn't pay its reporters well. Everyone except my mother worked there just long enough to get some published clips that would help them move up to a job at another newspaper and an online outlet—one that paid real wages. My father paid child support, but most of that money went into a trust fund in my name. I could access some of the money for college, but had to wait until age 25 for the remainder. I had no idea how much money was actually in there; my father was always tight-lipped about it. And when I asked my mother, she told me she didn't have any idea. But that couldn't be right. She at least knew how much my father agreed to deposit each month. A quick flash—did my mother use my trust fund for our trip? I push that question away. Knowing my father, he checked those statements weekly.

The buffet at Amour Café is good. Really good. Egg white omelet with fresh spinach, mushrooms, and a sprinkle of provolone cheese to hold it together. Still warm buttermilk pancakes with maple-cinnamon syrup. A blueberry scone, Greek yogurt with strawberries, and fresh-squeezed orange juice—the waitress made a point of telling us.

My mother raises her eyebrows when I return with my third plate.

"You don't have to…"

"I'm not trying to get my money's worth—I'm suddenly hungry!"

She laughs, pouring herself another cup of coffee from the carafe on the table.

"You're going to need a nice long nap on the beach!"

"Probably," I say, still chewing my scone.

"Want some?" she asks, holding up the carafe.

I shake my head and take the last bite, wondering if I should try a waffle next. Or a homemade glazed donut. Probably still warm.

I pause just long enough that my brain catches up with my stomach. I'm full. Too full for even one more bite of anything. Even a warm, glazed donut.

We're sitting on the outdoor patio of the Café, my mother with both hands wrapped around her warm mug like it's the middle of winter. It's in the low 80s, already. I'm thinking that's warm for the early fall here, but I don't know for sure and I don't feel like typing in "average fall temperatures in Myrtle Beach" into my phone. I'm just happy the sun is out and we're staying on the beach. Even if my mother is a drug addict. Even if she robbed my trust fund to pay for our trip. After living so simply for so many years, I probably wouldn't know what to spend my money on anyway.

"I'm going to sit here and make a couple of phone calls," she says. "Why don't you go upstairs and change into your suit?"

I'm already standing. "Should I meet you down here?"

"Yes, I need to finish the rest of the coffee," she says, picking up the carafe. "Wouldn't want to waste it. Have your key?"

I pull my phone out of one pocket, then check the other and slide out the key, holding it up as proof.

There's no one waiting at the elevator, so I'm back in the room to change quickly. I consider looking for my mother's bag-of-drugs again, but tell myself to leave it alone and read one of Miss June's letters instead.

After a string of ladybug inspired stationary, the next envelope in the stack is periwinkle blue, with a white lace design across the top. The flap is only lightly sealed and I pull out the matching paper inside.

Dear Anna Lee,

I have some exciting news. Exciting for me, but maybe you'll find it exciting as well. I have my own place. I loved living with May, but it was time to venture out. I'm not too far from my sister, just an easy 15-minute walk.

I'm living in a little townhouse and that same stream behind May's house runs through the back edge of my property. When I open my window in the kitchen, I can hear it. Of course, it's not grand like the ocean you so loved, or even the lake, but I think you'll like it.

I have an extra bedroom—you can pick the color and I'll paint it before you visit. There are two bookshelves in the room, and I've been filling them with some second-hand books from our local bookstore.

I'm hoping this will entice you to visit!

I have one more piece of news. I finally have a cell phone! Of course, you're thinking I was long overdue,

and you are right. My new phone is always with me, although I do put the ringer on vibrate when I'm teaching, sleeping, or in church.
    My love,
    Miss June

Across the bottom, she's written the number in large block letters. Finally. I pull out my phone, enter her under contacts as "June" type in her number, double check, and save. I could call her now. Or later tonight. Or tomorrow. It's going to be a long first call. Definitely not now. I put the letter back in the stack, throw my cell phone in my bag and pick up the key before heading down to meet my mother.

After a relaxing day on the beach, we're walking on the Myrtle Beach boardwalk, an area much different than the northern part of the town where we are staying. It's noisier and not as well-groomed. I see signs for bars and motorcycle rentals. And a tattoo parlor. My mother stares at the sign.

"Why don't we, Anna Lee?"

"Why don't we *what?*"

She's smiling, pointing at the sign. "Matching tattoos!"

I'm accustomed to my mother's spontaneous ideas, but this one is really odd, even for her. I laugh and keep walking. I turn and she's still looking up at the sign. I'm a half block away when I find a bench along the oceanside of the boardwalk. Carefully, I sit on the edge, my navy-blue shorts protecting my skin from the dirty, seagull-stained wood.

Tattoos. I've seen plenty of those in the area where I live. Even on a couple of my friends. My father once told me that tattoos were for *workers* not *professionals*. When I was younger, I didn't understand what he meant. Didn't professionals work?

Another example of my father's black and white view of the world. And as I look at my mother walking toward me, smiling as she's probably imagining our matching tattoos, I have another example of why my parents' relationship was never a real option. They would never have spoken again, I was sure, even if they ran into each other unexpectedly. Except for me.

"Oh, Anna Lee—wouldn't it be marvelous? Just marvelous?"

"Wouldn't what be marvelous?" I ask, already bored with this game where I pretend to not know the obvious.

She shook her head, her lips pressed together. "You know," she says. "The matching tattoos."

I have no desire for a tattoo, and even less desire for a tattoo that matches my mother's. I already know what design she'll pick before she says it.

"Coffee mugs! We could get coffee mugs to memorialize our quest!"

Too easy.

She is sitting beside me on the bench, and I didn't warn her about the sea gull droppings. And the splintered wood. Maybe if one imbeds itself in her thigh, she'll forget about the tattoo. Or remember how painful needles can be.

"I really think we should do it! Let's just go over and take a look at the designs."

I am certain of two things. Refusing will just make her sulk, argue, and sulk some more. And there is no way I'm getting a tattoo.

"I'll go with you. But no tattoo for me."

"But why?"

"I just don't want one. Why won't you let me make my own decisions?"

My mother smiles and springs from the bench. "I bet you change your mind."

As we walk away from the boardwalk, the area becomes less touristy and more unkept. I can't keep track of the cigarette butts, but count two condoms, five empty liquor bottles, and one pair of women's underwear. We pass a couple of bars with open doors, loud music blasting from one, the sound of arguing and clicking balls on the felt billiard table from the other. There's a closed check-cashing store and a nail salon with a front window so caked with grime that someone had written "dirty" with their finger, the *y* trailing off toward the street. Finally, the tattoo parlor. According to the sign–tattoos and piercings. Maybe my mother would get her belly button pierced. Or her nose.

Inside, my mother is already looking at the designs posted on the walls. Flowers, butterflies, sculls, crosses, wraps for the arms and legs. Nothing related to coffee.

"Hi ladies, I'm Kyle, one of the artists here," he says. "Looking for something specific?"

Kyle doesn't look much older than me. His head is shaved; he wears shiny-black framed glasses, and both of his arms are full of Army green, charcoal, and black tattoos—just designs, no actual pictures.

I wonder how long it took to cover so much skin. Days, weeks, years?

"Coffee mugs," my mother answers. "Is that possible?"

He's opening a large book on the counter. "It's possible. I think there's a couple designs in here."

On the wall, there's a whole section with Disney designs. Princesses, dwarfs, animals. Who gets these? Is there really a market for Disney tattoos? For adults?

"How about you?" he asks. "Looking for one of those? Let me guess—Belle?"

I laugh. "Don't think so."

"We're getting matching tattoos, my daughter and I."

I roll my eyes and shake my head. What would my father think? My mother was trying to turn me into a *worker*.

"She doesn't look so sure," Kyle says.

I give him a slight smile. Pretty smart. Despite all the evidence my father would point to on Kyle's arms, he seems more professional than worker.

My mother asks if custom work is possible. She's found a coffee mug, but she'd like a swirl above it.

"I could even spell out your names as part of the swirl."

"I love it! Don't you love it, Anna Lee?"

I don't love it. Now my mother is talking even faster than usual, trying to decide the best spot for the tattoo.

"I'd like it to show, but not all the time. Definitely not my back. Not sure about the arm, either." She turns to Kyle. "What about the size?"

"It's totally scalable," he says. "As large or small as you like."

She's lifting her right foot, tilting her leg to the side. Now the left leg. And repeat. "Hmmm, maybe just above my ankle. What do you think?"

"That's a popular placement for women," Kyle says, putting some sketch paper on the counter. "Anna Lee, right? And what's the other name?"

Back to the name idea again. "Jacqueline," she says, looking over his shoulder as he sketches. "Maybe smaller letters."

He's frowning, leaning over the paper as he draws. "Something like this?" he asks, holding the sketch in front of him. "What do we think?"

"Almost right. I like the two swirls, but I'd prefer one swirl, like our names are part of the same thread."

Kyle's sketching again, then raises the paper.

"It's perfect, isn't it, Anna Lee? Just perfect!"

Kyle looks in my direction. "Perfect for you?"

I laugh. "Well, it's perfect for one of us!"

"Not you?"

"Not me."

"I thought she wasn't sure," he says, turning back. "Solo tattoo?"

"She'll change her mind. Won't you change your mind, Anna Lee? It only makes sense if we *both* get tattoos. One day you'll be happy you got it."

"No I won't. I'll be happy I didn't get it."

Kyle folds the paper. "The girl knows what she wants—or doesn't want. Why don't you take this sketch in case you decide to get one yourself?"

My mother shakes his hand and lowers her voice. "We might see you tomorrow—I still think she'll change her mind."

It's going to be a long walk back to the car.

Chapter 28

My mother surprises me the next morning. She doesn't mention the tattoos. Before I forget, I pull out my journal and add the obvious:

#8 *My mother suggested we get matching tattoos.*

I had a vivid dream last night, in a big place with small rooms, each painted the same shade of blue. A place I've never seen before. A woman sat in the smallest room by the window, sheer curtains pulled back on one side. She was sewing a rag doll's arm back on its shoulder, using impossibly tiny, impossibly perfect stiches.

"It's magic," she said, seemingly reading my mind.

In the midst of the dream I heard my mother get up, banging her leg on something hard in the dark. I tried to stay awake, to see how long she took in the bathroom. To see if she was sick again from the pills in the plastic bag. The bathroom fan was noisy, with a metallic click sound every 30 seconds or so. I remember counting 11 clicks before I was back in the odd place with the small rooms.

I tried to see the woman's face, but she was bent over the doll, shoulders forward, shadowing the doll from the sunlight. The woman's arm had a mark, a red circle with a blue wavy line.

I floated from one tiny room to the other, but always returned to the woman and the doll.

In the morning, I tried hard to drift back. Is this a mystery I'm meant to solve? But it's gone, so I try to preserve it. Repeat the scenes in my mind. What was that on her arm? A tattoo? The sputtering coffee maker breaks my thoughts.

"You were smiling in your sleep, Anna Lee. Sweet dreams?"

"I think so. Did I ever have a rag doll?"

"Probably. Coffee before we check out?"

I wish we could spend more time in Myrtle Beach. But this trip could go on indefinitely if we extend our stays.

"Where are we headed next? Home?"

She pouts. "I thought we were having fun."

I don't respond.

She continues after a dramatic sigh. "Savannah. But we'll stop in Charleston on the way."

The drive takes a couple of hours. A couple of hours to think about what I'll say to Miss June and what she'll say to me. When I finally call her. There was a moment last night when I hoped my mother would get the tattoo. Then I could step outside to the street with the used condoms and empty miniature bottles. And make the call.

I play out different options in my head. One conversation where Miss June only asks about my father, another where she just wants to wish me well, or one where she begs me to move to Arizona. Or tells me I took too long to respond to her letters and she no longer cares about me. That doesn't sound like her.

How do I start the conversation? What would I say first? What would she say? It's almost a relief when my mother turns down the radio.

"Ready for a stop? I've always wanted to see the Angel Tree. Can you find out if we're close?"

I type in Angel Tree Charleston and a map pops up.

"We're close."

I turn up the volume and let the voice guide us to John's Island. We drive down quiet streets past houses with pretty flower gardens and children playing out front.

"Are we going the right way?" my mother asks. "Doesn't seem like there's anything back here."

"There's a marker at the end of the next street—looks like it's the right direction. What is it anyway? A coffee shop?"

"Oh, Anna Lee! It's a famous tree!"

I laugh. "OK, a famous tree. Why is it famous?"

"Maybe because it's over 400 years old."

"What does it *do?*"

My mother looks at me sideways and doesn't bother to answer. I see cars parked a short distance up the road. Looks like we've found it.

At every angle, the tree is impressive, but especially up close. I walk under the low hanging limbs, and immediately feel cooler. Its canopy of branches filter out the harsh heat of the sun while letting streams of light through. As I walk around, I'm stirring the dry dirt beneath, its earthy smell mixing with the sweet scent of the oak.

My mother insists we pose for a picture and hands her phone to a young black woman with tiny braids. When she hands the phone back, my mother smiles and says, "I like your hair," but the woman returns a strained smile.

I move to another spot and take a selfie with the tree. I might want to send a picture to Tanni when she returns from her trip. I've already taken a few pictures of Myrtle Beach to send her, including one of the *Tattoo and Piercings* sign.

There's a little boy with brown, curly hair wearing an *I'm a Pirate* t-shirt, grabbing one of the low-hanging limbs and trying to hoist his much shorter leg limb over, like he wants to shimmy up the mast to raise a skull-and-crossbones flag. An elderly woman in a tan skirt and stiff white shirt with a name-plate rushes over, taps him twice on the shoulder, and points to the sign. *No Climbing.*

I laugh. The boy is too young to read, but his mother understands. She's a few steps away, trying to navigate uneven terrain with a stroller that holds a younger version of the boy. She grabs the little pirate's arm just as he starts to raise his leg again. I can almost hear him say *Aargh.*

People are under and around the tree, talking, gathering for group photos. But it's quiet. Maybe the tree absorbs the sound as well as the light. Maybe that's why it's lived so long, refreshing itself daily with energy from the sun and the people who visit. A reverse sap. Oozing into the seasoned body and pulsing out to its limbs. Yet all I see are wrinkles, scars, aging. I wonder if the inside is unblemished and young.

The little pirate sharing its youth with the angel oak. Could a tree experience love? Could a tree give love, its branches covering all those who enter its space? Shel Silverstein certainly thought so in his book *The Giving Tree.* A nice thought. Maybe I was still mellow from my interrupted dream last night, the woman tenderly caring for a doll like it was alive, making surgical, magical stitches in its skin.

The water rises up in a wave from under the Jeep and splashes up to my window. I'm glad it's closed. We've veered off one of the main roads in the historic area, but the side streets are mostly flooded. Big storm? Water pipe broken?

Now we realize our detour is a dead end.

"Your map isn't working, Anna Lee!"

I shrug. The app has worked until this point. Maybe recent construction turned a through-road into a closed road.

"If we get back on the main road, it should reroute us. At least we know the general direction."

After two more splashes we're back on the main road, groups of tourists walking along the sidewalk. We are headed for Kudu Coffee. My mother promises that once she "refuels" we can visit some of the shops downtown. I look at the map I picked up from the gift shop at the Angel Oak. Ten art galleries and three bookstores.

It's a bright early-fall day but different than home. The leaves are mostly spring-green on the trees. Main street has better drainage than the side streets, and we turn towards Kudu.

"You can start looking for a spot," I say. "I think we're close."

Just a few vehicles ahead, a white SUV starts its maneuver out of its space at the curb.

"Right there," I point.

"I see it." My mother clicks on her blinker, a move my driving instructor called "showing intent."

An older black BMW approaches slowly in the other lane, then stops just in front of the exiting car. The blinker is on.

"Oh, no buddy—don't try it! I was here first." My mother rolls down her window and raises her hand in the air, waving it frantically. What kind of signal is that?

The BMW blinker turns off and the car moves forward. An older man with wavy gray hair slows down as he reaches us and rolls down his window.

"Sorry, Miss! Didn't see you there."

"No problem—hope you find an open spot!"

"I always do," he says, driving away with a wave.

"I shouldn't assume, Anna Lee. Let that be a lesson—don't assume!"

Not sure how I factor into the scene. I didn't assume. I figured the man was too busy looking at the parking spot to see her. Maybe this was her way of passing on a life lesson. Just living with her was enough of a life lesson. Of what not to do.

My mother is loud, attention seeking, irresponsible. Although way, way worse during her drinking years. Back then, she used the kind of language that would get me kicked out of school. She forgot to check my homework. Sign permission slips for field trips. Bake cookies for the class party. Make my lunch. Buy food.

We're walking toward the Kudu sign, spelled out in bright blue letters. Beneath, in much smaller letters is the rest of the name: coffee and craft beer. My mother won't be happy. Inside the plain brick front is a comfortable interior with a weathered, wood-panel bar on one side and tables for two along the windows that look out on the street. There's no line at the counter, so my mother has her drink in hand quickly. Nothing for me. Art galleries and bookstores don't usually permit drinks.

Back outside, she slips into the first clothing store we see. Flowing caftans, purses embroidered with flowers, and shoes decorated with glitter. My mother will be in there awhile.

I see an art gallery across the street and head over. The paintings all follow a coastal theme, but the approaches are unique. Brightly colored, almost cartoonish saturation by one artist, HD-photo accurate by another, and others that fall in the middle.

I'm in the second gallery when my mother sends me a text. She found a spa and is waiting for a manicure and a quick massage. She'll meet me in 90 minutes. Finally, it's the right time to call Miss June. It's a Saturday, so she won't be at school. I'm hoping she doesn't let all of her phone calls go to voicemail. She doesn't.

"Hello?" A single, lifted word. I forgot how much I love her voice. For a moment, my throat tightens. "Miss June?" even though there's no mistaking her voice.

"Oh, Anna Lee," her voice cracks a bit. "I knew you'd call one day."

She knows my voice. After all these years. I'm losing myself again, like I did in the gallery. I don't have to think about following any of the conversation options I considered. I give her a quick, but bright overview of my uninteresting life, and then tell her about the trip. She tells me a little more about her life. We both hold something back. I don't tell her my mother kept the letters from me. She doesn't tell me what happened with my father, why their marriage ended.

"How's your mother?"

"She's fine. Better. She told me about your friendship. Your music."

"I'm glad she told you," she said. "I miss it. The music and our friendship."

She's quiet for a moment. And I don't know what to say.

"Will you tell her? Tell your mother I miss what we had?"

"I will."

Before we end the call, she asks me two questions, her voice almost pleading.

"Do you promise to call me again? And will you at least think about visiting me in Arizona? You won't need any money—I'll pay for everything."

I agree, even though I'm not sure I'll follow through on the second request. The thought of telling my mother I'm going to see Miss June makes my mind race, and I look around for something to count.

Still my heart sinks a little after we end the call. Before the letters, I didn't know that Miss June missed me. So I didn't allow myself to miss her. Now there's that empty space within me.

My next stop is a vintage bookstore. Maybe there's a water-themed book on the shelves. As I open the door, there's a rush of scents. Mustiness tinged with something lighter. It's hard to break it apart, but there's mothballs and a tinge of salty sea water. And oddly, maybe a bit of bay leaf. Miss June always added precisely three whole bay leaves to the pot of red sauce before putting on the cover and simmering. I realize I'm among the cookbooks and I laugh to myself. Maybe someone used a bay leaf as a bookmark.

In each aisle, I scan my eyes over the titles, and lift out each book that stops my eyes, like a full sky with a single star that demands attention. For me, it's the author as much as the story so I turn over the book to read their bio. If I'm not ready to put the book back on the shelf, I read the first page. Always my deciding factor.

With no room in my suitcase, I'll need to be especially fascinated by any purchases. Although, I reason with myself that I can leave the books in the back seat of the jeep.

I continue to scan, lift, read until I have three books in my hand. One for me, one for Miss June, and one for my mother. The last one is a slim hardcover in excellent condition, although the sleeve is missing. A book of prose and poetry related to coffee. At the register, I ask the clerk to put the coffee book in another bag.

"Is it a gift?"

When I nod, she pulls out a small brown gift bag from under the counter, wraps the book carefully in white tissue, then adds a bouquet of red tissue to the top. Much better presentation than just a plastic bag.

We meet for lunch a few blocks from the bookstore. A place that smells like coconut, not bay leaves. My mother is already in the booth.

"For you," I say, putting the bag in front of her before I sit down across from her.

"A gift? How wonderful!"

She's carefully pulling out the tissue paper, and starting to unwrap the book when the waitress stops by.

"Can I bring you ladies something to drink?"

"We'll just need a moment," my mother says, eyes still focused on the tissue paper.

She turns it one more time to unveil the book, her mouth moving as she reads the title to herself.

"How lovely, Anna Lee! I can't wait to read this!"

She opens the front cover of the book and pulls out her pen, sliding both to my side of the table.

"Would you mind writing an inscription?"

I think for a moment and write: *To my mother on our quest for coffee,* then slide the book back. She reads it twice—I can tell because she mouths the words again.

"You don't know what this means to me, Anna Lee."

There are tears in her eyes, and my face grows warm. I only bought the gift for her because I bought a book for Miss June. But she doesn't need to know that. I decide to wait before telling her I called Miss June today. Before I tell her that Miss June misses what they had together. For the first time I can re-member, I really want my mother to be happy. It's a satisfying, but totally unfamiliar feeling.

Chapter 29

I practice my usual routine and leave my luggage by the coffee pots as I aimlessly walk around the lobby. There's a chart on the wall with the location of amenities. Laundry on the second floor—I'm overdue.

My mother is chatting a little too loudly with the man at the front desk, laughing, nodding, writing something. Probably recommendations for coffee shops. Or dinner.

She finishes and walks directly to the coffee station, her eyes focused on the target. I wait until she's stirring her cream before returning.

"I saw you by the brochures. Did you find anything you'd like to see?"

"I didn't look that closely. Lots of history, I think. Parks. Oak trees," I laugh.

"After the Angel Oak, I'm not sure we'll be impressed," she says. "We're in a good location. There are restaurants along the river we can walk to. Some live music outside."

The drive from Charleston to Savannah took us nearly three hours. It would have been shorter, but my mother insisted on deviating from the GPS. The waitress at the restaurant suggested a back road that was more scenic, but a longer drive. I'm ready to get outside and walk—laundry can wait until the morning.

After dropping our luggage upstairs, we pass through the lobby and out the rotating glass door to the street. The hushed sounds from inside transition to traffic and chatter on the sidewalk. My mother has a walking map in her hand, with restaurant and coffee recommendations highlighted in yellow.

The cars and people are moderate on the street by our hotel, but we walk two blocks and it's busier. Cars circling for on-street parking. Tourists walking, maps in hand. An occasional tour bus rolling by. We enter a carefully tended garden area and my mother's pace slows.

"Have you ever seen a mum this bright?" she asks, bending down for a better look at the almost neon yellow blooms. "I've never seen them this color at home."

She's cupping her hand under the blooms, and I'm instantly afraid she's going to yank the plant from the ground. But as quickly as she bent down, she's back up again, heading toward and down the stone steps to reach the Savannah River. Restaurants, shops, bars are nestled together, facing the water. Even more tourists here, many of them carrying drinks. I think my mother notices, too. She purses her lips and shakes her head when we pass a group of young women, drinks in hand, laughing loudly and faltering a bit on the cobblestone.

"Food first, and then a coffee?" she asks.

I nod. It doesn't seem that long since lunch, but my stomach says otherwise.

"I have some recommendations," she says, stopping suddenly and looking at the map. "What do you feel like? Seafood, Italian, Mexican?"

"I could go for Mexican. I'm ready for something different."

My mother looks up one side of the street, then turns to look down the other. She tilts the map 90 degrees, then looks back up the street again.

"I think it's this way," she says, motioning toward the area where we started.

"Why don't we ask someone?"

I'm surprised when she nods, and then approaches a college-aged boy on a smoke break outside a store. He points in the opposite direction. When my mother thanks him, he looks directly at me and answers, "No problem." He's not completely my type, but I smile back. He has light brown eyes and dark, thick lashes.

"Glad I asked," she laughs, as we continue down the road. "I really do have a terrible sense of direction."

Not news to me. Apparently, not news to her either. I always thought she was clueless about her navigation issues.

We hear the music before we see the sign. A trio of mariachi musicians are on the patio, with nearby hosts from other restaurants flashing menus and calling out cheerfully as people walk by. Fishermen all competing for the same finite number of fish. The river is a few steps away, but the fish they're luring are the ones on the sidewalk—the early diners.

Outside, only one table is occupied. It's a bit windy, so we sit inside at a table near the entrance where we can still see the sidewalk. I have visions of the musicians planting themselves at our table all evening, but they remain outside.

"I'm guessing you'd like some guacamole?" my mother asks.

The waitress arrives and places a basket of chips and a small black bowl of salsa on the table, and I don't wait for the guac. The chips are warm.

There's a break between songs and my mother leans forward. "Are you starting to enjoy the trip?"

Complicated question. My truthful answer is equally complicated, but I decide on something simple: what my mother wants to hear.

"I'm enjoying the trip."

She sits back, and tilts her chin up, looking at the ceiling, like her prayer has been answered. Fortunately, the conversation doesn't go any deeper. The waitress is back with the guac and ready to take our orders. We wave her off to look at the menu.

"Shrimp fajitas or shrimp tacos—can't decide," my mother says, tapping the edge of the menu with her index finger.

"Are you sure about shrimp?"

"Why?"

"It made you sick a few days ago."

My mother's face is behind the menu, and all I hear is "Hmmm."

"Didn't you say it unsettled your stomach?"

"Yes…but I'm sure it was a onetime thing. Maybe my system was out of whack with our travels."

I want to tell her I know it wasn't the shrimp; it was the prescription pills she's abusing. Instead, I let it go. I've all but made a deal with myself not to bring it up. Presently, things are pretty pleasant—I don't want to start an argument. Besides, I'll need her on my side if I want to visit Miss June. Although when I turn 18, I won't need her at all although that would certainly complicate my life. I'll have to come back home from Miss June's at some point. Or will I? The spring term starts the end of January and I should be in college by then.

Just the thought of school makes my heart start to race. I wipe my damp palms on my lap and take a long, slow drink of water. What was I so afraid of? Afraid that when I came back from school my mother would be an alcoholic again? Along with her drug habit? Afraid my father would just set up a cot in his office and never return home? Afraid they'd both forget about me?

I put down the glass and the waitress is staring at me. She looks impatient. She doesn't even ask if we're ready, just pulls out her pad and pen from the apron and leans forward. My mother doesn't order shrimp. Chicken fajitas. When it's my turn I say without a trace of malice: "Shrimp tacos, please." My mother starts to open her mouth then snaps it shut.

The music is loud inside, even though the musicians remain outside playing to mostly non-customers. The sun is starting to set and the people are almost in silhouette as they pass along the riverfront walkway. I see a small figure skipping, two people holding hands, someone carrying an umbrella overhead even though it's not raining. Still, the scent is in the air.

"Sorry, I have my nose in my phone tonight," she says. "The editor has some questions about one of the stories I filed before I left. Needs to check the sources."

"Why? Are they afraid they'll get sued?"

"Of course there's always that, but they want to be sure the story is right. Fairness. Accuracy."

Her phone dings again and she's staring at the screen.

"No—that's not right," she says as she types, and then suddenly stands. "I'm just going to call. This could go on all night."

I nod and she's still looking at the phone as she walks outside, passing the musicians until she's silhouetted and then completely out of view.

My mother usually wrote stories about fundraisers and profiles about musicians and artists. Maybe she named the wrong winner for our county's annual pie bake-off. She was back as quickly as she left.

"What kind of story is it?" I ask.

"It's a series, actually. A series of articles about people in our community who are overcoming addiction."

Interesting.

"What kind of addiction? Drugs?"

"All kinds, I hope. I've written three so far, and the first is scheduled to run this week. The name of the doctor was misspelled during the first edit. They tried to call the doctor to confirm his quote, but couldn't locate him. Wrong spelling."

"So what have you written about so far? I mean, the kinds of addiction."

"The first was alcohol. I thought it would make sense to start with something I knew. The second drugs, the third gambling. I have a contact for the next article on shopping addiction."

"That's a thing?"

"It is."

"What kind of drugs...for the person you wrote about that is a drug addict?"

"He's a recovering drug addict. Mostly heroine at the end, but other things along the way. He's only 23-years-old, but he's already lived a long, heavy life."

She draws out the last three words slowly, then takes a deep breath.

"Do I know him?"

"You don't. He's from Maine."

"But he's living in Jersey?"

"Yes. He's burned a lot of bridges in his short life. He's moved from his mother's to his father's to an aunt's, and then to a sympathetic cousin's house. He lied to them. Stole from them. He had a stepbrother who lived in New Jersey who offered to get him into a rehab. It was his one option besides living on the streets, so he took it. Turned out to be the right choice—at least for now."

"Don't you think he's going to make it?"

"It's day by day, Anna Lee. It's not just one right choice; it's a thousand right choices. I hope…I'm praying he makes it."

It seems like just a few days ago my mother was talking about that herself. How she was still tempted. I wonder if writing about the addicts was hard for her, or if it was a kind of therapy? Was it her idea to write the series, or the editor's?

I see a lightning streak break the sky in two parts, and hear a combined "Oooooh" outside from the crowd. The musicians are mid-song, but they step just under the roof, playing with a little more volume and passion. A family and two separate couples walk up to the hostess. It was probably the threat of a storm, rather than the music that brought them inside, but I see the tallest of the three musicians smile broadly at the other two. Maybe they were paid a commission.

I don't hear the waitress behind me and I jump slightly when she reaches around with my plate.

"*Lo siento*," she says, putting a hand on my shoulder, before switching back to English. "Anything else?"

While we're eating, three more groups enter and I can't help but count the tally for the musicians. How much commission could they make? It couldn't be much. Maybe a dollar each? I count the number of people—18. Probably a dollar a person. Split three ways. Now I'm overly curious about the commission, but I'm not going to ask. Besides, what would I ask? Would I walk up to one of the musicians and ask if they received a bonus for every person who enters?

The waitress has just cleared our plates and I remember my conversation with Miss June.

"I finally called her."

"Who did you finally call?"

"Miss June."

My mother's face snaps back a little, her eyebrows raised. "I'm glad, Anna Lee. I hope she's doing well."

"She is. Working at the school in Arizona."

My mother nods then drains her glass of ice water.

"She actually wanted me to tell you something."

"Oh," she says. "That's surprising—after all this time."

"She wants you to know she misses what you two had—the music, the time together."

My mother sits back, her hand over her mouth. "That's not what I expected," she says quietly.

The waitress is back with the check and our conversation ends as my mother adds cash to the billfold before handing it back.

We're heading toward the door, past the musicians who are playing for a family of three at another table. Once we're back on the cobblestone walkway the rain starts, but it's slow and measured. I can almost see the clouds opening to send down one short stream at a time. We press on. We're back up the stairs and walking away from the hotel, toward one of the city squares. The streams of rain are thicker now, but we're under the trees, the moss dripping off and across, like a wide umbrella. But one with a pinhole leak that lets an occasional drop slip through, but not enough for us to really care.

"Should we keep walking?" my mother asks. "Make it to the next square?"

"Let's."

Just off the next square, there's a covered patio with a musician playing guitar and singing "Take it Easy." We find a bench under a big oak—it's less wet than the others. The weather is cooler now, and I'm wearing a sleeveless shirt. But it's so calm and pretty outside. A crescent moon. Tiny white lights on trees in front of the businesses. Old-fashioned globe streetlamps. And the smell of rain mixed with fresh cut grass. We listen to another three songs before my mother stands.

"It's mystical out here, Anna Lee. I'm glad we're seeing Savannah at night."

She hooks her arm in mine as we step down to cross the street, and I don't pull away.

Chapter 30

I surprise myself by rising early. My laundry is already finished and it's only 8:30. My mother has a recommendation for coffee and breakfast that's just a few blocks from the hotel. The rain is steady and we huddle under a small, travel-sized umbrella. Our arms brush, our feet wet as we splash through dips in the sidewalk.

I'm closing the umbrella and see two open high-top tables, so we continue past the "seat yourself" sign to the one closest to the window. The coffee smells wonderful, even to me. My mother is already looking around for a waitress. We don't wait long, and she delivers two huge white mugs on our table before we even ask.

"Did I get it right, ladies? Coffee?" she asks, as she places a small metal pitcher of creamer on the table next to the sugar bowl.

My mother laughs. "That obvious?" She glances at me. "Would you bring a cup of ice for my daughter? She prefers her coffee cold."

"I'll be right back with ice and a couple menus."

I'm discretely looking at some of the plates around me to see what looks good. We're both hungry, so when the menus arrive, we make quick selections without discussion, and our orders are on the way to the kitchen.

"I think last night was my favorite part of the trip," she says. "So far."

"It was a beautiful night. And speaking of *so far*, how much further are we going?"

I wanted to ask *how much longer are we going to be on this trip*, but focusing on the distance seemed gentler.

"Let's not worry about where we're going, Anna Lee. Let's just enjoy our time together."

She's pulling out the Savannah map as she takes a sip from her coffee, moving the mug next to me, then unfolding the map across the table.

I want to tell her I'd enjoy the time more if I had a general idea of how long this was going to continue. But I don't.

We spend another half day in Savannah, walking through other city squares, while my mother tells me for the third time there were once 24 historic squares, but now there are a total of 22. She literally memorized the travel brochure.

We've already checked out at the hotel and I'm waiting by the empty bellman's station as my mother gets "one for the road" at the coffee station in the lobby, then chats with the front desk clerk, a sullen-looking woman with short, curly brown hair and glasses who's probably a decade older than me. When I first see her, she looks like it's the worst day of her life. Within a few minutes, she's laughing with my mother.

"It's not that bad!" the woman laughs. "Really not that far at all. Let me print off directions for you."

My mother is striding toward me with a crooked smile.

"OK," she says, pulling the handle on the coffee carafe, even though she just filled the cup. "How does Hilton Head sound?"

"Didn't we…"

"Yes—we did. But it's not much of a backtrack. Maybe an hour. Could be even less if there's no traffic."

"Does that mean we're headed back up?"

"To the hotel room? We're already checked…"

"No—to Jersey. Back up the coast?"

"Oh, no–our trip isn't over yet! Just a short backtrack. We'll keep going down south," she said, her hand playing with my hair. "Don't worry!"

No end in sight. *That* was something to worry about. I thought about telling her, but instantly imagine her pouting, tears forming in the corners of her eyes. I keep my mouth closed and follow her to the car. In a few minutes we'll be leaving the parking lot, my mother turning up the music louder than necessary. Before she asks, I'll start looking up coffee places and hotels in Hilton Head. Coffee places first. I'm fully aware of my mother's priorities.

Hilton Head is completely different than I expect. First, there are other hotels beside Hilton. Second, none of the buildings are very tall. Third, there are streets filled with houses. I wonder if people actually live here year-round, or if these are vacation homes for rich families. Or, maybe these lovely houses are rentals, made lovelier by bright pink flowers with yellow centers, wide-leafed palm trees, and front porches with outdoor furniture that's way nicer than what we have inside our home in Northern Beach.

There's another surprise in the car. My mother doesn't turn the music to her usual volume. Maybe she wants to talk about the trip. Or unveil her drug problem. But the only time she speaks is to double check directions. And even then, her voice is at a five level, not her typical 10, or 12, or 22.

The sun is reflecting off the windshield, and she lowers her visor.

"I don't have a reservation, but it's a weekday, off-season. Shouldn't be a problem. You pick."

"We're spending the night?"

"Sure, why not?"

There's no end in sight. If my mother had a pressing appointment back in Jersey, Hilton Head would be a day stop, then we'd drive to the next location by nightfall. What's the next location? The ultimate location? The source that's funding this trip? Maybe my mother's office Powerball pool finally hit. They've been playing steadily over the years; it's bound to happen. Unless you actually consider the odds.

I don't really care where we stay. So I start to count hotels. Unless it's hurricane ravaged, I'll pick the seventh hotel. The Omni is the winner.

My mother seems brighter when I point out the selection, but still not her usual HD brightness. The salt is in my nose when I step onto the parking lot. There's a firm breeze and all the palm trees are leaning right.

The lobby is empty and we're in our room quickly.

"There's a coffee and donut place that looks good," I say. "Duck Donuts. But it's inland. We might need to drive."

"I'm okay," she says, looking distracted. "Why don't you go down to the pool. I have a few work calls I should make."

Before I leave, she hands me a $20.

"In case it takes longer than I think, get yourself something for lunch at the pool."

I start toward the door, then turn. "A key?"

She just stares at me.

"In case I need to get back up? The bathroom?"

"Oh. Well, there's a bathroom by the pool, I'm sure," she says, pulling the key card out of her purse. "Here."

She doesn't want me to come back up, but why? Maybe she really does have a lot to discuss with her editor. Or she has some questions for one of the people she's writing about—the addicts. The *recovering* addicts. Or maybe she's making a call to get more prescription pills overnighted to her.

I'm almost out the door and she says, "Why don't you call your father?"

I stop the door before it shuts. "Really? Why?"

"Just to check in. Have you talked to him since we started our trip?"

"No—not sure he expected me to. And he's at the office."

"He'll take your call, Anna Lee. He's probably worried about you."

I slide my hand off the door and hear it click behind me as I turn the corner for the elevator. I doubt my father has ever worried about me. But if he knew my mother tried to talk me into a tattoo…I'm still smiling when the elevator doors open.

"Someone looks happy to be at the beach!"

There's a man about my mother's age smiling back at me. He's wearing a white button-down shirt and bright teal tie with tiny coral sailboats.

"You don't look like you're headed to the beach," I say.

"I will be! Gotta get some business out of the way first."

At the lobby, he extends his hand forward. "Ladies first!"

There it is again. That same sweet scent I've noticed in every oceanfront hotel. I wonder if that manufactured scent can cover up unpleasant beach odors—rotting fish, mildew. I stop to fill up a clear-plastic cup with strawberry-infused water and take two cucumbers for my eyes from the bowl filled with ice. Might as well enjoy the full Hilton Head experience.

It's my lucky day. No children at the pool. There are only two women sitting side-by-side with identical tans that indicate they've spent a lot of time in full sun. I move down to the other end, facing the ocean. As I settle back, I realize there's a palm tree trunk in my line of vision. I get up and move three chairs to the right. Perfect view.

My father. Once my mother has something in her head, she'll continue to ask me. I pull out my phone and his secretary answers after the second ring.

"Hi Carol, it's Anna Lee."

"Well hello, Anna Lee. I hear you're on quite some trip with your mother. Drinking lots of coffee are you?"

"Someone is drinking lots of coffee. Not me."

She laughs. "I'm putting you through to your father."

Carol has worked for the company as long as I can remember. She's more like my father's work *mother* than work *wife*. He'll be lost when she finally retires.

His voice sounds rushed when he answers. "Is everything alright?"

"Yes…why wouldn't it be?"

"No, I mean of course."

"She said I should call you, so I'm calling you."

He takes a deep breath into the phone. "Are you enjoying yourself?"

I talk longer than I planned. Tell him about our route, the Angel Oak, Savannah's City Squares, the art galleries, great donut place, the beaches. I don't tell him about the tattoo parlor or my call to Miss June.

Right before we hang up, my father asks, "How's your mother?"

I'm not sure how to answer, because I'm not sure what he means. Is he wondering if my mother is driving me crazy? Is he wondering if my mother *is* crazy? Is he genuinely asking about my mother because he cares about her? I remember that call between my parents at the beginning of the trip. My mother laughing, tilting back her head.

"She's fine," I say. Even though I'm not sure that's true.

I'm at the end of a nap and not ready to open my eyes until my shoulders start to burn. I look from one side to the other and confirm—sunburn. I remember applying lotion to my face, neck, and chest. Did I apply it anywhere else? Definitely not my shoulders. I slip on my t-shirt, determined to at least prevent it from getting worse. I realize the women at the other end are gone and the pool bar to the left, empty when I arrived, is now half-filled. I squint to see the clock over the bar: 2:00. I've been asleep for three hours. And my mother is nowhere in sight. I pick up my book from the patio where it fell, page now unmarked, and return it to my bag. I step into my flip-flops and stand, automatically placing the bag on my shoulder, then prying it off gingerly. I hope my mother packed aloe.

I expect to see her by the coffee station in the lobby, but she's not there or at the front desk, so I take the elevator to the third floor.

There are three housekeeping carts in the hall, and when I arrive at 310, I see the "Privacy Please" hang tag on the door. I slip in my key and it lights green.

The room is dark. Maybe my mother walked to a coffee shop. I almost turn around but decide to use the bathroom first. And when I come out I see her—asleep on the bed. She's lying on her back, right on top of the palm-tree bedcover.

"Mom?"

I repeat three times, each time a little louder, but she doesn't move. The drapes are closed tightly, so I pull the cord and the sun streams right across her bed. She doesn't react. I think something is seriously wrong with my mother.

I step close, touch her shoulder, and shake it slightly, and she startles awake.

"Anna Lee, you scared me," she shouts with a frown.

"Sorry. You were out pretty good."

She sits up and looks at her phone on the bedside table. "Are you kidding me—2:17? How is that possible?"

I shake my head. "Someone must have slipped something in our last drink," I say. "I fell asleep at the pool. Any chance we have aloe?"

She heads into the bathroom without responding. I look through my own bag, even though I'm sure I don't have any in there.

After a few minutes she steps out and says, "Aloe—I think so," like I just asked her.

As she roots around in her small case, I can hear the pill bottles clicking around. Or at least I think I can. She's raising up a bottle in the air. "Aloe! Wait—why do you need aloe? Did you forget to use lotion? That's why I remind you so much…"

"OK! It's just my shoulders," I say, with a dramatic sigh to imitate my mother's usual response. She shakes her head, but motions for me to sit on the bed, so I carefully pull off my t-shirt. She drops aloe on my right shoulder and the coolness is immediate, like opening a freezer door on a hot day. With the gentlest of strokes, she applies a thin layer of gel before moving to my left shoulder.

"I hope that doesn't blister," she says, her voice scolding, like I'm 8-years-old again. "Better for you to stay out of the sun for a few days."

"Are we heading home?" I ask, keeping my voice even so I don't sound so joyful.

"Of course we're not ending our trip, Anna Lee! There's more to vacation than the beach. We'll just plan our route accordingly. We haven't even checked out a coffee shop in Hilton Head yet—I bet they have some nice ones."

"And bookstores?"

"Of course they have bookstores. Why don't you change and I'll see what I can find out at the front desk? Join me downstairs when you're ready."

Once she's out the door, I remember the pills clicking in her bag. I pull out the plastic bag, hidden under her smaller makeup bag. This time I count—seven bottles. Without opening, I can see half of the labels, and they all have her name. At least she's not stealing from her friends' medicine cabinets. They are all from the same doctor, a name I don't recognize. And all filled at our local pharmacy.

There's a loud knock at the door and I jump, but manage to slip the bag back to its original place as the door opens. It's a young woman about my age wearing a faded blue uniform.

"Apologies," she says, in a heavy Spanish accent. "Do you need towels?"

"No thank you, we're fine."

Probably better that I didn't have time to fixate on the bottles. I'd be looking up each of the prescriptions on my phone, an hour would pass and my mother would be back upstairs. I try to imagine her face if she came in and caught me. She'd be shocked, angry, confused. But the only face I can picture is one of relief. Maybe that's her last secret. And the trip won't end until she tells me.

I'm down the stairs and out through the lobby door when I see her at the front desk, chatting away, making arrangements for this evening, for tomorrow. Maybe for next week. Or maybe for next month. How long will she hold out before telling me? How long will I hold out until I confront her? I'm not likely to find any answers soon.

Chapter 31

At some point, I realize it's a dream, but I keep my eyes closed so I can find out how it ends. A man is shouting. Shouting so loud that I keep my head down, hidden in the shadows, hoping he loses me in the dark. But he's standing right over me, so I try to sink lower. I'm on the floor, my head pressed so tightly I smell the oak planks. Louder and louder, even as my hands cover my ears. The man is leaning closer, so close his hot breath is on my neck, his spit on my cheek. I can't make out the words, but somehow know they are inflicted to make me ashamed. I will myself to open my eyes. And just before the dream ends, my head raises slightly from the floor and I see tiny braids. The girl is not me—it's my mother.

Still groggy, I instinctively know the man is my grandfather, my mother's father. Nothing my mother did was good enough. And never would be, so she left him, left her home. Left the place where she sat in her mother's lap as she read her books. Laughed and sang. Kissed her. The place that still held her mother's scent. Left the town where her mother was buried.

The pain in my shoulder brings me back to the hotel room. But it's not the sunburn that keeps me frozen in bed, it's a realization. My mother is still running. Running from a ghost now, but one that is real to her. How could I help her stop?

For years, I thought my mother's drinking was a way to hide from her failed relationship. Or her responsibilities to me. She was hiding. But not from my father. And not from me.

She's still hiding. Those pills in the plastic bag. If I had thrown out the bag when I first discovered it, it wouldn't have mattered. She would have found another way to hide.

I'm out of bed and in the bathroom when I hear the door open, and I smell coffee, strong coffee.

"I have a green tea for you," she shouts. "Iced. Thought you might feel like something cool this morning."

When I finish, she's standing by the glass sliders to the balcony. She's still looking at the ocean when she says, "Let me get some aloe on that burn."

I'm ready for my tea, and it's perfect. Cool, refreshing. Maybe I should pour some over my shoulders.

"Come here," my mother says, turning toward me. "Let me take a look at that sunburn in the light."

She stretches the corners of my short sleeves with her fingers and raises the material carefully so she doesn't touch my skin.

"Mmmm, okay," she says, lowering the sleeve back down gently and moving to the other side. "Well, I'm optimistic. I don't think it's blistering."

"Does that mean I'm clear for the beach?" I ask.

"You're clear for the shade. Maybe a beach view, but definitely the shade. With your shoulders covered. But I've got a list of indoor places you might like."

Before I have a chance to ask, she continues. "Including two bookstores."

She slides open the door to the balcony. "Full shade. Let's have our drinks out here and enjoy the view."

The clouds are stark white against a medium blue-gray sky. We both see it at once.

"Doesn't that..." I start.

"Look like a camel," she says, pointing.

We laugh. It's distinct—the neck, face, hump.

"Anything else up there?" my mother asks, taking another sip of her coffee.

I think I see a tree, but my mother sees a giraffe. There's another formation that resembles a bench, or a hard chair, but my mother doesn't see it.

"There's a bell," she says suddenly. "Reminds me of the big brass bell we had in the center of town. We only had one town square but it was pretty—paths that wound through the garden. Nearly every lady in town was part of the garden club. Each spring they'd add bulbs to the tulip beds. In the late summer they were out there pruning the roses. I suppose they were there year 'round. Seems like each time I passed there were ladies with wide-brimmed hats kneeling by the flower beds."

"I didn't see any bells in Savannah's city squares. Why was it there?"

"You know, I never thought to ask."

"Do you miss it?"

"The bell?" she asks.

"Your town. Where you grew up. You must have a lot of memories there."

She's quiet and we both focus on the waves. Four ins, four outs before she speaks.

"Good memories. Bad memories. Not much in between."

"But do you miss it?" I ask again.

"I try not to think about it. Too painful."

"The bad memories?"

"The bad memories and the good—painful for different reasons."

I know it's time. But I count another ten ins and outs before I ask.

"Can we go there?"

My mother looks at me, her eyebrows raised. "There's nothing left there for me. I said goodbye to that town a long time ago."

Five ins, five outs.

"I'd like to go."

Five ins, five outs and she's quiet. Looking down at her coffee.

"It's important to me. I'd like to see where you came from. Where you lived."

And silently I add, "And why you keep running."

As we drive further from the coast, the clouds break up and drift off, leaving nearly unseen wispy outlines of where they'd been just seconds before. Just two hours earlier, I was pulling dusty books off the shelves of the used bookstore in Hilton Head. The books were not gently used. Some of them were so weathered I wondered if they were first editions. Doubtful. I carefully turned yellowed, slightly brittle paper to read the first line or two and walked out with two new purchases. The opening lines in both books made it onto my list. I pull out my book journal, the one I've been keeping throughout high school, and turn to the back where I've written my favorite beginnings, from the first pages of books. A few of the best, from my view:

It is a truth universally acknowledged, that a single man in possession of a good fortune, must be in want of a wife. (Pride and Prejudice)

When he was nearly thirteen, my brother Jem got his arm badly broken at the elbow. (To Kill a Mockingbird)

Mr. and Mrs. Dursley, of number four, Privet Drive, were proud to say they were perfectly normal, thank you very much." (Harry Potter and the Sorcerer's Stone)

Sometimes, it was a simple phrase that captured my attention, like "want of a wife" or "thank you very much." Other times, it was a single word or a name. I'd never known anyone named Jem.

I've been a list-maker my whole life. My mother still has what she believes is my first list—a checklist I wrote to prepare for the first day of second grade. There are four items on the list: Pick out clothes. Do hair. Fill backpack. Make lunch. My spelling wasn't quite so accurate on the actual list, but even today the last item makes me sad–I already knew my mother might forget to pack my lunch.

I remember the coffee journal, take it from my bag and write:

#9 Drove across six states just to see an old tree.

How was that for an opening line? Would I read the rest of the page, the chapter, the book? Probably not. If this were a book, I'd need a more dramatic start.

He was older than anyone I knew, but in a flash I saw a child climb on him and nearly sever his brittle limb.

Better. I look at my previous addition to the journal.

#8 My mother suggested we get matching tattoos.

Definitely room for improvement.

Walking over used condoms, liquor bottles, and dirty underwear, my mother insisted we get matching tattoos.

Sensational, but accurate.

The Jeep windows are down, the wind rushing through. I pull my hair back and offer my mother a band, but she shakes her head. Her braids whip front, back, sideways as we drive, and she's singing louder than the loud music.

Our last stop in Hilton Head is a coffee shop. Watusi. My mother sees the saying, *it is what it is* on the sign and knows she's picked the right place. She'd often use those words when I complained about something that couldn't be changed. I wonder if the restaurant is telling us we'd better be happy with our order—because there'd be no changes.

We sit at the U-shaped bar area in the front where a few scattered singles are eating either a late breakfast or an early lunch. The mixture of the scents—citrus, berry, egg, cheese, coffee—makes me instantly hungry, and we decide to order lunch before our drive. The Farmer's Market sandwich sounds good to us both, and big enough to split. *Grilled eggplant, tomato, marinated portabella, fresh spinach, avocado spread, drizzle of extra virgin olive oil on warm Cuban bread.*

After we place our orders, my mother sees someone come in from outside and hops off the barstool to take a look at the patio seating, then asks the waiter if he can bring our food outdoors.

We sit at a round, white iron table, shaded by the umbrella, sipping our coffees—mine an iced latte, my mother's traditional.

"I bet this is what Paris is like," she says. "Sitting outside sipping coffee."

I laugh. "I think there's more to Paris than outdoor cafés and sipping coffee."

"Of course. I wish I'd gotten to Paris."

"You haven't been anywhere in Europe, have you?"

"No, and Paris has always been at the top of my list."

"Maybe when I graduate from college, we'll go together."

My mother takes a long, slow sip from her coffee and doesn't answer. Maybe she thinks I'm being sarcastic.

"No, really. Wouldn't that be a great way to mark my graduation?"

"It would be, Anna Lee. It definitely would be."

She's looking to the side, like something important requires her focus. But when I turn, there are only empty tables.

"Let's just concentrate on this trip," she says quietly, turning back to me. "As they say, it's the journey, not the destination..."

We're back on the interstate, wind rushing through, loud music and I'm thinking of my mother's words: *it's the journey, not the destination*. Maybe it's a combination of the two. It's the journey that's leading us to our next destination, the one where I can finally learn more about my mother's upbringing. I'm still surprised she agreed.

My assumptions have already been tossed aside. I always thought she was raised in a free-spirited family. Hippie parents.

I'm tired, but not ready to close my eyes. Maybe I'm afraid that the man in the dream will appear again. Now I'm wondering if it was a mistake to force my mother back to the place where he lived.

Chapter 32

"Do you have a way to contact your cousin?"

We're only 15 minutes outside of Midville, now on back roads, the interstate routing us to the closest exit.

She turns down the music. "I do—I have her number. Once we find a place to stay I'll give her a call."

Farmland frame both sides of the road. On the right, tall stalks of corn, with a single stalk at the end rising above the otherwise uniform level. On the left side, plants spread closer to the ground, maybe lettuce. We drive for another mile and the right-side changes to peach trees. I see civilization ahead on the left–plain wood houses close to the road with a small shopping center and a gas station.

We stop to fill up and my mother is nodding when she gets in the car.

"We're going in the right direction. There's a military base near here, so keep an eye out for some hotels."

We drive a few more miles when we spot a sign for the Midville Hampton Inn and follow the sign to the right.

"Are you sure you don't want something in town? Maybe near the town center? It sounds so pretty."

"No, Anna Lee—I'm sure. This is close enough."

Maybe my mother is protecting her dreams, like the closer she is to life with her father, the more likely he would invade her dreams. If it weren't for my own experience, I would have counted her fears as more evidence that she was crazy. Now I wasn't so sure. Unless I was crazy too.

"We'll get settled and then I'll try to call Belinda. Maybe she'd like to meet us for dinner."

This is the one destination where I hope she takes some extra time—time to get past what she's been avoiding.

"We will get to see the town, right?"

"Yes, Anna Lee. We'll see the town."

"And your house?"

"We'll drive by. We drove four hours to get here; we can see whatever you like."

The woman behind the desk is the friendliest person we've met yet. Back home, I would have been suspicious of her. Her accent is heavy, so I find myself reading her lips. I'd never heard an accent in my mother's voice until this moment. When she responds back, there's something extra, something slower. Like all the other secrets in her life, she hid her own natural voice.

My mother hands me a key card.

"Room 522. I'll be up after I call Belinda."

The accent is gone.

I hope she isn't going to pretend she's calling her cousin, then tell me Belinda can't make it. Even if my mother reverts back to her full, natural accent, I'll still be suspicious.

The coffee pot is straight ahead when I walk into the room. It's the kind with pods and there's a selection of flavors. She'll be happy. We're nowhere near the ocean, but I still pull back the curtains to see the view. A car dealership in the distance and lots of farmland. There's a shiny red barn and a simple white wooden house. Both look like they've just been painted. Best part of the view—someone's on the front porch sitting on what I imagine to be an Adirondack chair. The lake. Miss June. We still have so much to talk about. Maybe more depending on what I learn from Belinda. Assuming my mother actually calls her.

I consider reading more of Miss June's letters. Instead, I pull my book from my bag and settle back on the celery-green, stuffed chair in the corner. I'm half-way through the chapter when the door clicks open.

"Yes—coffee! We're not at the beach, but at least there's coffee!"

She's already sorting through the flavors. "Can I make you a cup? Bold flavored, breakfast blend, vanilla? You could get some ice from the machine by the elevator." She's holding a pod in each hand, like she's weighing her choices.

"No, I'm good." "Did you reach her?"

"What?"

"Belinda?"

"Oh, yes," she says, putting the winning flavor in the machine and taking a cup into the bathroom. "She can meet us for dinner," she shouts above the running water.

"I'm sure she has a lot to tell you."

"Maybe. You're surer about that than I am," she says, pouring the water and starting the coffee maker. "Not sure how well she actually knew him."

"Well, you'll know after tonight."

"I suppose, Anna Lee. I suppose. We've got a couple of hours. I might take my coffee to the lobby, make a few work calls. Do you want to bring your book downstairs?"

"I'm fine here. Probably quieter."

I turn back to my book. There's a lot happening in the storyline, but I can't help but think that tonight's story will be even more fascinating.

We're getting in the car when my mother finally speaks. She's been unusually quiet on our walk downstairs.

"Belinda suggested Jasper's Grill. I think you'll like the location—it's right in the center of town. I guess you'll get your first glimpse tonight," she says quietly.

"Don't you want me to see it?"

"Well, *you* want to see it. And so you will."

I want to point out that her mother lived here too. And didn't she have many happy memories with her? Instead, I open the app on my phone and start the route to Jasper's. Just a six-minute drive. I turn up the volume to let my phone navigate–I don't feel much like talking myself.

We both took extra time to get ready for dinner. Neither of us has been wearing much makeup on the trip. Even my mother's usual heavy coating of red lipstick has been missing lately. I'm wearing the one sundress I packed. I never expected to wear it, but my mother made the purchase for me specifically for our vacation. It's mostly yellow and white, but at least the trim is aquamarine. My mother hasn't deviated from her usual dress code—bright pink top and full skirt with large pink and purple flowers. Peonies, I think. Just like the ones in front of our public library.

We find a spot at the curb, just a half-block from the restaurant. It's dusk, but the city square my mother described is just across the street. Through the trees, I can see the bottom of the bell she described.

"We can walk over there after dinner," my mother says. "It's even prettier at night."

We're walking with matching strides and I'm half anxious, half excited. I wonder what my mother is thinking. There's a woman standing in the front—tall and blonde like my mother. She's smiling as she walks toward us.

"Why Jack-a-lyn, darlin'! You haven't changed a bit. Not a bit," she says, her accent prominent, slow, and drawn-out. "Well, maybe your hair–but I love it!"

She and my mother hug and they both turn to me. Before my mother speaks, the woman is hugging me. "I'm so happy to meet you darlin', Anna Leeee! So, so happy you're here."

Her enthusiasm is as overwrought as the woman at the front desk of the hotel. And once again, the accent is reassuring. Besides, she's family. No reason to be suspicious.

As soon as we settle at the table, Belinda has more to say. Much more. My mother isn't expecting to learn anything new about her father. I'm glad her expectations are wrong. We barely touch our food and my mother never requests a coffee refill.

Belinda picks up the timeline from when my mother ended her contact—after he didn't show up for graduation.

My grandfather's drinking continued to grow worse, especially after he was forced to retire from teaching. Belinda's mother, Catherine became his caretaker by default, a role that I'm sure would have fallen to my mother if she had stayed in town. Twice, Catherine found him unconscious in the house after failing to reach him by phone. After the second time, she "bullied him into detox and rehab." And not just any rehab. My grandfather had received a sizable inheritance from his uncle, money he invested that grew even more sizable. Enough that he could use a portion of the money for six months of in-patient rehab at a place clear over in Atlanta.

"This was a no-foolin' place," Belinda tells us. "We visited him after two months and thought he would drop out, or get kicked out at any time. Each day my mother waited for a phone call. We returned the next month and couldn't believe the change. We thought he might be fixed, ready to go home. But he was clear—he was in this until the end."

Belinda shows us pictures from those visits. I looked back at the man who had been a mystery all my life.

The man in Belinda's photo had dark, cloudy eyes that stared straight at the camera lens, like a mug shot. He was frowning and the corners of his mouth reached down slightly, a convict who wanted to be set free.

She shows us the second picture—although just a few months later, he looked much younger. A decade at least. He had a tentative smile, like he knew freedom was in reach. But not yet. My mother returns the first photo to Belinda. She holds the second one and asks, "May I keep this?"

Belinda nods. "Before he came home, he actually asked Catherine to go into his house and throw away all of his bottles of gin and whiskey. He told her about all of his hiding places— the nightstand, the cabinet under the bathroom sink, the china cabinet. Behind the textbooks on the shelf of his study. And a half-bottle of vodka in the freezer. Lots of hiding places and lots of alcohol."

I couldn't help thinking about my mother's own purge— telling her friend about the hiding places.

He stayed in a sober house for another three months, not far from the rehab. My mother is shaking her head. "My father?" she asks.

When he returned, he volunteered at a state-run facility in Asheville, helping with intake. Later he tutored men there who'd dropped out of high school, working on math and reading skills to help prepare them for the GED.

"Did he ever talk about my mother?" I ask, even though I was afraid of the answer.

Belinda takes a breath. "Whenever my mother and I asked him if he'd tried to reach out to you, or if you'd reached out to him, he only had one response: 'She deserved so much more.'"

My mother made a soft bird-like sound that I'd never heard before as she starts to cry. I take her hand in mine and she looks at me, her face twisted.

"We were hoping you'd somehow hear about the funeral, that you'd come back. Some of the men from rehab were there, others from the sober house. Two of the young men he tutored spoke. One of them went on to college. First a Bachelor's, then a Master's degree, and your father met with him every week, all the way through until his graduation."

I try to imagine the man in my dream as someone who became generous, caring.

"Would you have come back, Jack-a-lyn? If you knew he'd changed?"

It takes my mother a long time to answer. "I don't know, Belinda. I don't think *I'd* changed enough to come home."

My mother hugs Belinda for a long time before we leave. On the street, my mother takes my hand without a word and we cross into the garden. Strands of globe lights spin like an illuminated web overhead, reflecting off the broad-leafed trees and changing hues from dark to light green as the breeze starts and stops and starts, the web pattern like lace on the path. We sit on a bench and my mother points to the bell.

"It's still there," she says. "The whole town has changed; there were small businesses on the other side when I lived here. A pharmacy, a woman's dress shop, an appliance store—all family owned. Now there are these restaurants. It's all changed, but the bell is still here. I'm glad for change, but I'm glad something remains. It's good to remember the past. You don't have to stay there, but it's good to remember."

I know she's not talking about the bell anymore.

Chapter 33

"Are you ready?"

We are finishing breakfast downstairs at the hotel, and my mother is standing over me.

"You don't need another coffee refill?" I ask with a laugh.

"Well of course, I need another refill! I'll get one for the road right now."

My mother is taking me on a tour. She's promised to show me her town, or what remains of it.

"Be patient with me, Anna Lee. You know I haven't been here for over 20 years. I hope I can find my way around."

I have no choice but patience when it comes to my mother's direction-finding abilities. Besides, I'm looking forward to seeing where she grew up.

We're in the Jeep and the music is noticeably off. But my mother fills that space with chatter. Excited chatter. One-hundred-heart-beats-per-minute chatter.

"See that corner right there where the bank is now? That was a little pizza place—Tony's. I went to school with the owner's son, Michael. He worked there part-time. Always gave us extra pepperoni on our slices when we stopped by on the weekend."

"And that corner with the gas station," she continues. "That was a county office where we used to pay our water bill each quarter. The lady behind the counter kept a jar of lolly-pops and always remembered my favorite was green."

"The laundromat is gone. Used to be right there by the county office."

"Didn't you have a washing machine?"

"Yes, but not a dryer. At least not for a long time. My mother would hang out clothes on the line, but when we had a run of bad weather, she'd just take everything down to the laundromat. We'd walk over to the bookstore and sometimes I'd take my allowance to buy something."

"There's a bookstore?"

"End of the next street."

But as we drive toward it, she starts to pout. "It's gone. It was right there—right where that real estate office is."

We navigate a few more streets, and she makes a U-turn. "Sorry, things look a bit different now."

She makes another turn, then bounces on her seat.

"Oh! The library is still there, but bigger! They must have added on. I wonder when that happened? Let's go in."

We park on a big lot out back and walk up the steps, my mother thinking aloud about what's changed.

"I don't see the book slot. Oh, there it is! Still in the same place. I think they added on to the right side—the brick looks different. And these benches—also new. How nice—the garden club is sponsoring a community herb garden. Look at that sign, Anna Lee! *Bring your scissors for a tasty dinner.*"

Inside there's a rush of book-like scents. I wish someone would make a candle to capture that distinctive aroma.

My mother walks directly to the counter, but I decide to take a tour, walking past the display of "autumn reads" for adults, the second display of "staff recommendations" and a third display of "new bios." I circle through fiction, then non-fiction, and end up at the back of the library in the large children's section. The colors show a distinct change from the rest of the library's subtle shades of blues and greens. Here, there are bright primary colors—small blue plastic tables with red chairs, a chalkboard with listing of new books by ages, and six bright yellow bean-bag chairs arranged in an arc in front of a hard-backed black chair. It all looks like a preschool classroom. I loop through and move into the young adults' section. A disappointing two cases, with four shelves apiece. Maybe the kids were like me and graduated straight from children's chapter books to adult novels. Or maybe they just stopped reading. I hope not.

I walk back slowly, and my mother's still at the front desk. There are three women talking with her now. Two are much younger, but the third woman looks about my mother's age. Maybe they went to school together.

"Let me introduce you, Anna Lee," she says, "This is Suzette. We grew up together."

She extends her hand and I take it.

"Your mother and I rode our bikes to the library when we were in elementary school," she says. "And I remember her fondness for Nancy Drew mysteries–she read and re-read every book on the library shelves."

No wonder she bought me the full set of those books one year for Christmas. My favorite present from her. With the exception of children's stories and self-help nonfiction, the only time she bought me books. Even though I asked for specific titles every year.

"And this is Jess and Amanda. They didn't ride their bikes with me to the library," she laughs and the women laugh loudly like she made a hilarious joke.

My mother invites me to join her and Suzette for a coffee in an hour. They're already talking about coffee shops, and I wonder if my mother can wait that long for her next cup. I sense an opportunity. She agrees to drop me at the hotel first, then drive back and pick up her friend. Seems like the perfect time to give Miss June another call. Or read a few more letters. Or both. I'm surprised I don't feel the same longing, the drive to reconnect with Miss June again. Maybe because I've already connected. Or maybe because my mother is starting to seem a little more rational. Or at least, a little less crazy.

Chapter 34

I drag the chair to the window even though there's no ocean view. The lighting is diffused. Wouldn't have been a great beach day, but perfect for reading without a glare on the page. The next letter in the stack is a card. A birthday card with two bright blue Adirondack chairs beside a slightly lighter blue lake. There's a hand-drawn book on one of the chairs, with the title written in script: *Anna Lee's Birthday Tales.*

> *Happy 14th Birthday, dear one! I hope you do something perfectly wonderful on your day. I'm reminded of our days on the lake, reading passages to one another. Do you remember? I hope we can have such a day here in Arizona. I have the perfect place. There's a grove of pines along the river, with a cut out just wide enough for us to spread a blanket and enjoy the shade and scent of the trees, the sound of the flowing river just loud enough that we'll need to raise our voices a little when we read.*

I close my eyes for a minute. So many days at my father's house on the lake. How many? I wish I'd counted. If I'd known they were going to end, I would have counted for sure. The sun on our faces, swatting away an occasional fly, shadowing the book by tilting our heads forward to block the sun. Looking up to identify our favorite bird couples—the cardinals and the blue jays.

It's time to call Miss June again. Her phone goes to voice mail, so I leave an awkward, quick message. She's probably still teaching. I pull out the next letter. More memories. More of Miss June telling me how much she misses me. Loves me. I've read four more letters when she returns my calls.

There's a bit of small talk and a moment of quiet that goes a little too long, so I tell her.

"The letters were kept from me."

I can't bring myself to directly implicate my mother, so I take a passive approach. Miss June doesn't want to implicate her either.

"I'm sure your parents had their good reasons. It was a hard time. They didn't want to confuse you even more. They waited until just the right time. I'm glad they waited until you were ready."

My parents. I'm fine to let my father absorb half the blame, even though it's likely he was never aware of them.

We talk about my trip, about the current destination.

"I'm glad she went back there, Anna Lee. Your mother never wanted to talk about her hometown, but there were times when she shared a little. Very little. And always with such sadness."

"She didn't want to come here. I sort of insisted."

"You always had good instincts, even as a young child. I bet those instincts are even stronger now."

I mention the birthday card she sent. Ask her about the place by the river.

"I was just there a couple of weeks ago. It's so lovely and no one seems to know about it. I've never seen a single soul there."

We talk for almost an hour. Past, present, future. A visit to see her.

"I can make your reservation and get the information to you the same day. Just let me know when you want to come."

I promise to send her a few pictures. As soon as we end our call, I'm scrolling through my photos. I send her three. My favorite shot of the ocean, three hues of green and two blues in wide bands that stretch to both sides. A picture of me on the Myrtle Beach boardwalk that my mother took, the clouds pink behind me. And the Angel Oak, it's brittle, sprawling limbs silhouetted on the dusty ground.

Within minutes, she's responded with a text: *Your call and your pictures made this a special day! I am crying over how beautiful you are, Anna Lee!*

Once more, I realize how much I wish Miss June was in my life. I try not to fixate on how many years it's been, how many moments gone. She said *they waited until the right time.* A generous statement. One that didn't factor in selfishness.

I'm putting my phone away when I hear another text, but it's not Miss June this time.

Did you miss me? Back from Italy! Following my Instagram???

Tanni. Instagram. I'm the only person my age without Instagram. Although if I'd realized Tanni would be posting pictures there, I would have loaded the app. Everyone we knew would have known, except me.

I also didn't realize how much I missed her until now. Just like Miss June, although the time away from Tanni was weeks, not years. Maybe I was even more hopelessly introverted than I thought. That trait didn't come from my mother. Definitely my father. Could my parents be more opposite?

Tanni and I exchange a string of texts and pictures. I send her all the shots from Myrtle Beach, along with the tattoo shop picture and a description of the matching tattoos that never happened.

My mother returns, apologizing as she walks through the door.

"I certainly didn't intend to be this long—we had a lot to talk about! Are you starving?"

She doesn't wait for me to answer.

"The good news is—I have three great restaurant suggestions. You decide."

She tells me the names, one at a time, and I'm looking them up. I give her my choice and she sighs.

"Oh, I was hoping you didn't pick *that* one. The only thing is…"

I give her the name of my second favorite, and make a mental note to add to my journal later:

#10 Tells me to pick a restaurant and she hates my choice.

After a good night's sleep, we're on our way out of town, but my mother wants to see one more place. The house where she grew up with her mother. And father. I'm surprised, glad, nervous. I hope this doesn't set her back. She drives by the house quickly, her eyes starting to water. Then she circles the block and drives by a second time, more slowly. At the end of the block, she pulls to the curb and shifts the Jeep into park.

"Will you walk with me, Anna Lee?"

We're out of the car and she has a commentary for each house, starting with the gray-blue Colonial on the corner. She pauses in front like she's conducting a tour.

"The Hudsons lived here. Miss Anna, Mr. Bob. They didn't have any children, but they had a sweet little terrier named Molly. Miss Anna would knit little sweaters for Molly—long before that was a thing. On hot days, my mother would fill an old plastic bowl with water so when they walked up to visit, Molly could cool down."

We move to the next house, dark green with a long front porch and a V-shaped peak just below the roof.

"There were three different families who lived in this house. I didn't know any of them very well. One of the women who lived here was pregnant, and I remember my mother taking her some children's picture books as a gift."

The tour continues with a story connecting my grandmother to each house. Baking bread for the Weaver family when they moved into the brown Tudor, delivering a meal to the white house with the black shutters for Mrs. Hammond after she miscarried her baby, weeding the side garden of the stately white home with columns after the elderly, widowed Mrs. Harris broke her hip. "The garden was right outside her bedroom window and she could see it from her bed."

We are now seven houses from the corner. The house we came to see. The house my mother tried to forget for her whole adult life. She is standing in front of it, and suddenly she stops talking.

The house is plain and small, especially compared to other houses on the street. It's a standard wood Cape Cod with no enhancement. No front porch. No pillars. No special trim. Wooden window boxes minus flowers. But the color is spectacular. A custom sky blue without discernable gray.

The landscaping is minimal, mostly azaleas whose blooms are long past, leaving green leaves heated to a crispy brown. There's a one-car driveway, but instead of a car, there are chalk drawings–a yellow sun, blue and red balloons, an orange cat-like creature—all sketched with thick, wobbly lines. A child's bicycle with a white basket on the front is tilted over in the grass. Green-sparkled streamers flow out of the handlebars—like fireworks that will never project into the sky.

"How does it feel?" I ask. "I mean—how do you feel?"

"Not like I thought I would."

"Better? Worse?"

"Different. I feel different."

She's still looking straight ahead. I wonder if she's trying to remember something, or trying to forget. To leave some of the memories here, lay them down and walk away so she never has to think about them again.

"He was sorry," she says suddenly.

"Your father?"

"He said, 'she deserved so much more.' I take that as an apology. And I accept it. And I forgive him."

She's laid it down. Left it. And she's returning to the car. I take five big strides to catch up with her.

"I'll tell you one thing my father did, Anna Lee. One good thing, and he doesn't even know it."

"What's that?"

"He made this trip possible. Our journey. After he died, I received a check. I didn't even know what to do with it, didn't know if I wanted it, but I put it in the bank. He's paying for our trip."

I don't know why, but I send up a little thank you to my grandfather, then I cross one worry off my list. At least my mother isn't selling prescription drugs for travel money, just holding on to those pills for herself. I suppose it's too ambitious to think she'd reveal more than one secret today. At least we're down to one. Next time I'm in the mood to count, I'll figure out how many she's revealed.

We're getting in the car and she's already shifted her attention.

"How's your sunburn today? Ready to head back to the beach?"

Chapter 35

Florida. We're heading to Florida but there's no specific town in mind. And for the first time since I grudgingly left New Jersey, I'm okay with that.

When my mother asked, "Do you think we should dip into Florida before we head back home?" I was excited, although not openly. I'd only been to Florida once, but I was too young to remember much. My mother participated in some newspaper conference in Orlando, and she brought me along as well as her friend Edna who watched me while my mother attended her sessions over the weekend. We spent four days at two parks—Disney and Epcot.

There's a photo album my mother keeps on the coffee table at home filled with pictures from the trip—530 pictures total. Six of me posing with Mickey, two with Minnie, one each with Goofy, Snow White, and Cinderella. Eight of me on the carousel atop a horse with a silver mane, two on the Dumbo ride, eleven at different locations on Main Street. There are fourteen pictures of me taken at Epcot, mostly in the International Section. My mother told me that Mexico was my favorite.

I'm also excited there's an actual end coming to our trip. And for some reason I can't pinpoint, I'm glad the trip isn't ending just yet.

Before we left Midville, my mother suggested we stop for lunch, pulled out the map the woman at the Hampton Inn printed off for her, and came up with a plan. Or at least my mother's version of a plan.

We're back in the Jeep once more, and I realize I'm not even looking for something to count.

"We'll take as many stops as we want on the way," she says. "There's no rush."

Ahhhh. She's still doesn't want our trip to end.

"After we pick a beach, let's find a really great place to stay. We still have more of my father's money to spend," she says, smiling.

"Are you trying to spend it all?"

"Why not," she laughs. "We'll look for something with *resort* in the title. *Oceanfront resort.* Maybe a suite."

She really is trying to spend it all. Maybe that was part of letting go. Letting go of the house, the money, the past.

"Do you think you might get in this time? Get in the ocean?" she asks slowly, like she's afraid to hear my response.

"Maybe...not too far in…"

My mother is smiling broadly. "Proud of you, Anna Lee."

She sees a hamburger stand at the end of the block on the right and gestures.

"Sure–fine with me."

I sit at one of the empty picnic tables, closest to the ordering window and we look at the menu on the building, deciding on two breaded chicken sandwiches.

"Coffee?" she asks.

"Only if they have iced."

I'm looking at the map when she returns from ordering.

"Here's our number—not that we need it," she laughs, looking around at the empty tables. "They'll call us when our sandwiches are ready. No iced coffee, but there's a place just a couple blocks up the street. I'll be right back."

"No really, that's fine. I'll just take something else. Or a cup of ice to add is fine."

"I need to stretch my legs anyway. Almond milk?"

"If they have it. Otherwise a little cream."

She removes the lid from her coffee and takes a little sip, then straightens quickly. "Too hot! Too hot even for me. Might melt my lipstick," she laughs. "I'll leave this here until I come back."

The road noise is loud and I wonder how healthy it is to eat food while surrounded by emission fumes. I can't help myself. I count five trucks—one with chicken, two with furniture, two unmarked, before turning my attention back to Florida. I'm considering a few beaches and cross-checking the distance on my phone when I hear the signals for two texts. Miss June and another from Tanni. Must be good reception at the hamburger stand. I reply to Miss June's first—she wonders how the rest of the trip back to my mother's hometown went. There's a string that follows, and Miss June says she's happy my mother was able to visit her house. *I know that must have been hard for her.* And I respond, *hard but good. She seems happy.*

I'm moving to Tanni's text now and I hear a sound. Three sounds—two machine-made, one human. A squeal, a thud, a scream. Then a second scream by a different voice. A minute goes by and the traffic starts to slow, then back up. I hear a siren first, then see the reflection of red lights on the shiny metal *Dixie Foods* tractor trailer.

I hear the girl at the window calling "Number 5 is up" as I start running toward the sounds.

Chapter 36

My mother's been gone eight months. The distractions help me forget. Arrangements to make, people to notify, more arrangements to make. It's how I avoid thinking about her loss, what her loss means to me.

She was hit by a truck. A *Farm Fresh* tractor trailer swerved right to avoid a car entering too quickly from the left. The police officer on the scene told me the intersection had one of the highest accident rates in all of North Carolina, a blind spot caused by a large oak tree on the corner. It was over 100 years old, and discussions about taking it down always ended with *no*. The tree was still there, thriving.

Why did my mother have to be there, at that intersection, at that precise time? It was her constant search for coffee. That damn quest. Only this time, it wasn't for herself, it was for me. She wanted me to have an iced coffee.

My mother's connection with strangers was returned to me that day. The truck driver involved in the accident, an elderly woman, a young girl who worked in the coffee place my mother never entered. They stayed with me, called my father, made me drink water, sit in the shade. The elderly woman held my shaking hands and hugged me while I cried. The policeman took me to the station and later to the airport to meet my father. I don't remember if I thanked any of them. I don't remember if I thanked my mother when she insisted she get me an iced coffee.

I'm living with my father now. He's decided not to put my mother's house on the market just yet. I've been there exactly four times. Once to gather up what I needed—clothes and other essentials. A second time to pick up a few more items— mostly books. And the last two times to take everything from my bedroom. Stuff I didn't even remember I had. Stuff that reminded me of my mother. Most of those items are still in boxes, stacked in one of my father's many spare bedrooms.

I've waited months to look through the rest. It's late spring, and today, I'm starting what I expect will be a long process of going through my mother's belongings. I insist on going by myself and my father gives me boxes to collect everything I want to keep. I tell him one box will be enough—I can't think of anything I want. But he gives me six, "just in case."

Before I go inside, I walk slowly around the outside. I expect to see her beautiful gardens overrun with weeds, but the flowers have pushed through. Orange day lilies. Bright yellow daffodils. White, lilac, pink tulips. The rose bushes budding. Our already massive mimosa tree has fanned out and buds have formed. My mother looked forward to the feathery pink flowers each June. There's not a weed anywhere and fresh mulch covers the ground. Someone has been tending her gardens.

When I enter the house, my mother's lilac scent is gone, except in the bedroom, where the closed door entombs her presence. Her bright, pink and red floral quilt is spread neatly, the coordinating pink bed-skirt beneath. Five pillows are on top–two in the quilt design, two rose-shaped and rose-colored, and a small oblong purple pillow with yellow glitter writing that reads *Life is Good*. I place that pillow in my box. On her bedside table, she has her favorite coffee mug. It's pale pink with a Robert Browning quote: *the best is yet to be.* Another item. That's two. This first box still looks pretty empty.

I slide open the drawer of her bedside table and pull out a small square box covered in shells, the kind you can buy at any beach town souvenir shop. The shells are yellowed and some pieces are broken off. I gently open the lid. Poker chips? I turn over the first. Of course. Her whole collection of chips from AA, ranging from one month to seven years. I line them up in order on the bed, trace my finger over the designs. Did she do the same? Tracing her fingers over them each to congratulate herself on a successful day, and remind herself of what it would take to be successful tomorrow. Courage, hope. Life-changing achievements that I knew nothing about. My mother came to every award ceremony at the school, even when I insisted my only award was a certificate for perfect attendance. I replace the chips and add the shell container to my box. Also in the drawer—a fringed royal blue shawl that she wrapped over her shoulders when she wrote on her laptop in bed, and a folder with medical records. I placed the sweet-scented shawl in the box, using it to cushion the mug and the shell box. I leave the folder in the drawer before closing it.

My mother's scent is now part of the box, and I put the lid on snugly to hold onto it a little longer.

There's no one outside when I leave, and I open the back of the Jeep, carefully setting the box inside. I was in the house for about 10 minutes. When I go again, I'll try to make it to 15, maybe 20. Maybe I'll fill the box next time. I'm certain there will be other surprises.

Even with all the secrets my mother shared on our trip, she had one more. She was already dying. The truck unexpectedly ended her life a little sooner, but it was likely she wouldn't have made it to the next summer. Cirrhosis of the liver. Her earlier addiction to wine was on track to take her life even before coffee gave her a new, healthier obsession. Those moments of illness during our trip—she must have known her time was growing short.

The secret I thought she was keeping from me had an explanation. She wasn't addicted to pills. Prescription medicines managed her symptoms, but probably weren't going to give her what she wanted most—more time.

I'm making more lists now. The counselor my mother's friends urged me to see suggested I set goals and make lists. To make some progress each day, no matter how small.

Today's list:
- Collect my mother's mementos.
- Research two college classes that interest me.

Tomorrow's list:
- Start a display of my mother's mementos.
- Sign up for classes.

The counselor said I should take things slow for the first year, so I am. Not expect too much of myself. Not expect too much of the people around me.

Miss June calls me every evening. Sometimes we talk for 10 minutes, other times for more than an hour. I'm planning to visit her in the summer. She's offered to fly out to New Jersey, to rent a hotel room for the weekend so we can spend time together. I'm not ready. She even offered to come out for my mother's service, but it didn't seem right—to either of us.

I'm not mad about the letters anymore. Strangely, I do think my mother gave them to me at the perfect time. Instinctively, she knew that after her death, Miss June would be important to me. And she was willing to let that happen—to even orchestrate it.

My mother was cremated, and according to her instructions, no viewing or burial. But there was a celebration service at our little church. I expected my father and a few of my mother's friends, maybe some of her coworkers. The news staff and editors were there. But there were others. I didn't expect to see my friends, most I hadn't spoken to all summer. And my teachers. I suppose my mother was memorable to them. There were business owners and other people from the town my mother had written about. Isabella and Marlissa, owners of the second-hand shops my mother frequented, were there. I noticed they both wore outfits that would have been in my mother's collection. Maybe they had been holding those clothes for her.

I exchanged handshakes and hugs with friends of my mother—people I'd never met. Many friends from AA told me how much my mother had inspired them, kept them on track. A young man wearing a too-loose, wrinkled white shirt and too-short navy tie told me between tears, *your mother was a lifeline for me.*

"She interviewed me for a series she was writing on recovering addicts. We met for coffee and I thought that's all it would be. A one-time thing. But she gave me her number, told me I could call her anytime. And she *meant* it."

He said he'd talked to her several times while we were away. I think those calls she made to her editor on the trip were really to him.

Belinda came with her daughter and two other distant cousins who had never met my mother. *I'm so glad we reconnected, Anna Lee. I felt an instant bond with your mother. She was such a darlin' person.* Was. Each past tense was painful. But a little less painful than the time before.

Everything about the service reminded me of my mother. The red and pink roses on the altar. The hopeful scripture readings. No one giving sad eulogies or wearing black. Even songs she would have picked. Because she did. She left an envelope with instructions with the one person I never expected. My father. He was the only person she told she was dying.

He never said why she told him. Maybe she wanted him to prepare to take a bigger role with me. To do more than bring home carryout at the end of his long workday. He's trying, even agreeing to attend a couple of my counseling sessions with me. "Whatever you need, Anna Lee." He uses the phrase a lot. Last week he took a half-day off. We picked up sandwiches from the deli where I used to work and ate them at a picnic table at the beach. That was his idea. After, we went to the used bookstore—my idea. He asked me for a recommendation, and I found a well-read copy of Sherlock Holmes and the Hound of the Baskervilles. I hoped my analytical father would connect to the great detective. Now in the evening when I sit back in the soft leather chair, he sits in the matching chair with his new book. My father reads just one chapter a night before placing the complimentary bookmark at the start of the next chapter.

"I'm already up to chapter six," he told me last night.

I held back a laugh. "It's fine if you want to read another. Don't you want to find out what's going to happen next?"

"No, no. I want to make it last."

I decided not to tell him there were other Sherlock Holmes books. Next time I'm at the bookstore, I'll pick up a few so he'll have new options when he finishes.

I've spent a lot of time in the Adirondack chair, identifying all colors of the lake. Sometimes on cloudless days, I've seen a band of ultramarine along the far edge. It's funny that I never noticed my favorite color on the lake before.

My mother was a complicated person. I learned more about her on our trip than I did the prior 17 years. And I knew

I'd continue to understand her in the days, months ahead. Although it would be years before I was grateful for her. Grateful that she was my mother, instead of Miss June.

In my mother's *effects* presented to me by the police officer, I found her journal. I haven't read any of her writings yet. I've added a few items to my journal, but with more context and gratitude. But I kept what I'd previously written. I wonder how many of her crazy behaviors I would grow to miss?

I already know what my last item will be, and I think my mother will like it. *Gave her life to buy me an iced coffee.* I'll write it one day. But not today.

Acknowledgements

To Tony, Sarah, and Christa, whose constant encouragement emerged from the purest of motives—they knew publishing a book would make me happy. To my son-in-law Alex whose creative advice saved me needless legal worries. And to my sisters Nancy and Gail who have known me the longest and love me despite my flaws and the fact that I am the tallest.

My sincere thanks to first readers Cindy Jamieson, Danielle Duprey, and Nancy Stancill, whose keen eyes found discrepancies I missed. Their feedback lifted me to think I might actually publish. Appreciation for thoughtful edits from Chris Goss—she made me realize (among other things) that dropping commas was acceptable. For advice from writers Linda Murphy-Marshall and Mary Ellen Porter-Grady, and to all my previous print editors, especially Marc LeGoff. To Adelaide Books for believing in my work.

To all at the University of Tampa MFA in Creative Writing program—thank you for enriching my literary life. Special appreciation to directors Dr. Erica Dawson (present) and Dr. Steve Kistulentz (past) who crafted and cultivated a dynamic program, and to Lynn Bartis who managed all the moving parts. For mentors who helped me find my voice—Tony D'Souza, Dr. Donald Morrill, and especially John Capouya whose guidance helped me transition from my journalistic style.

I'm forever grateful to all of my fellow Tampa classmates whose courageous writing made me realize that mine will never be that brave—but I'll keep trying. My book was improved by my alumni workshop group—Gerry Winter who read cover-to-cover, and by Beth Engelman, Amanda Phoenix Starling, and Camile Araujo who reviewed one or more chapters. And for Tanya Adams Guillory (my Tampa bestie), Faby, Vicky, and Katie—other incredibly talented UT alum whose kindness and support inspired me to improve my writing.

And finally, to my parents whose love still makes all things possible, and to my God who opens my heart a little more each day.

About the Author

Donna Koros Stramella is a writer from Maryland whose fiction and nonfiction pieces have been published in Adelaide Literary Magazine, Scarlet Leaf Review, Columbia Magazine, and the Baltimore Sun. She is a previous award-winning journalist and a graduate of the University of Tampa MFA in Creative Writing. She is the author of a novel, *Coffee Killed My Mother* and is working on her second, *Among the Bones*.

Photo Credit: Larry Bowers Photography

Topics and Questions for Discussion

1. How would you describe the relationship between Anna Lee and her mother? Does the relationship between mother and daughter change during the story?

2. What did you like and/or dislike about Jacqueline? Would you consider her a strong or weak woman?

3. What prompted Jacqueline to plan the trip? Why do you think it took her so long to be honest with her daughter?

4. June was an important part of Anna Lee's childhood. Did June do enough to continue her connection with her step-daughter? What steps might you take in similar circumstances?

5. Was it appropriate for Jaqueline to hide June's letters? Why or why not?

6. How has her father's addiction affected Jacqueline? How has Jacqueline's addiction affected Anna Lee? Discuss real-life examples of the impact of addiction on other family members.

7. Although Jacqueline has hurt others, she holds onto some bitterness. Does she find forgiveness on her journey? For whom?

8. At one point, Anna Lee is excited to think Miss June might be her real mother. Do you think Anna Lee's feelings continue or change by the conclusion of the story?

9. Is Anna Lee an unreliable narrator? Why or why not?

10. At the end of the story, how has Anna Lee changed? How has her father changed?